Rette could see Jeff Chandler leaning forward . . .

his eyes on the speaker, his lips slightly parted, as though he were hanging on every word.

"Wings Airport," Mr. Irish announced, "is willing to give a course of flying lessons to any student sixteen years old or over who can qualify. The course will be offered as a prize in a contest."

Those few words in Avondale High changed some lives—*Lorette Larkin,* star of the girl's basketball team; *Jeff Chandler,* editor of the school paper; *Elise Wynn,* lovely and popular. This is a story of today's high school crowd; in particular the story of Rette Larkin who says:

"And suppose I don't especially want to be a lady?"

A Girl Can Dream

BY BETTY CAVANNA

Cover design by Charles Beck

A TAB CLUB BOOK

Published by the Scholastic Corporation, publishers of
Scholastic Magazines. Distributed by the Teen Age Book
Club, 33 West 42nd Street, New York 36, New York

CHAPTER ONE

Loretta Larkin stood with her hands thrust deep in the pockets of her tweed reefer and stared into the window of the Avondale Book Shop. Stinging February wind whipped the edges of a plaid scarf wound around her head like a nubia, and her feet, in thin-soled loafers, were so cold that they ached.

Valentines, sentimental or frivolous, half smothered the book display, but Rette wasn't attracted by their legends. She was thinking that a book—if she could find the *right* book—might do.

Impulsively, Rette decided to go inside, but the moment she opened the door she was sorry. There was such force to the wind that it pulled the knob out of her hand and sent the door crashing against a book-stacked table. Then, when she got behind to push it closed, the wind capriciously abated and left Rette's shoulder braced against thin air.

Bang! The noise of the gale was shut out, and within the store there was the unnatural quiet of a public-library reading room, with Rette feeling, through no fault of her own, like the proverbial bull in a china shop.

"Goodness, it is windy, isn't it?"

A solicitous young clerk came to help her gather up the fallen books, but the girl's very effort to put her at ease embarrassed Loretta further. She could feel herself redden as she restacked the books awkwardly.

"It really is," she said.

The clerk didn't ask Rette if she could help her. It was a shop policy to let customers browse. Besides, most of the high-school crowd came in only for valentines these days.

But Rette stood for a while before the shelf marked "TRAVEL," then moved to "HOBBIES," and finally approached the dark-haired girl, who looked more collegiate than clerkly. "D'you think you could suggest something for me?"

The girl smiled. "Are you looking for something special?"

Rette nodded, her gray-blue eyes sober. "A book for my brother. For a birthday present. I don't know if there'd be anything—" She paused.

The clerk's glance roved toward the children's shelves. "How old is your brother?" she asked.

"Oh, he's not a kid!" Rette burst out. "He's twenty-three. He was in the war."

The pretty clerk looked amused at her own mistake. "Well, in that case, what is he interested in? Biography? Fiction?"

"He doesn't read much," Rette admitted, frowning because she wasn't sure a book was such a good idea after all. "He's interested in flying, mostly." Her shoulders straightened proudly. "He was with the 82d."

"The 82d Airborne?"

Rette nodded.

"What's your brother's name?"

"Tony Larkin."

"Oh, I know him! At least I've," the clerk corrected herself as though she had been overassured, "met him. We were on a double date once."

Rette looked more carefully at the girl. Goodness knows

it was to be expected that anybody close to his age in Avondale would at least have met Tony Larkin. He'd always got around.

"Well, it's for Tony I want the book," Loretta said abruptly. "But maybe there isn't anything—" She was more than ever sorry she had come in here. She had no words to explain to this girl who knew Tony that it couldn't be just *any* book.

"And he's still crazy about flying?" The clerk was moving thoughtfully up and down the aisle between the tables and the shelves. "Is he working at it now?"

"No. He's selling for an oil company." Rette wished it didn't sound so prosaic, so unlike Tony. "But it's flying he's keen on, still."

The girl pulled down a book and handed it to Rette. "I guess he'd have read this?"

Loretta looked at the title—*Wind, Sand and Stars*. By a man with an unpronounceable French name. "I don't know," she said.

"It's tops, but it isn't new. Still, if he doesn't read much—"

Loretta was riffling the pages. Suddenly she felt incapable of ever finding a proper present for Tony. This book or one of a hundred others—how could she ever decide?

"If he has read it," the clerk suggested, "he could exchange it."

You'd like that, Rette thought jealously. You'd like to see him again. She was at once proud and resentful that girls always felt this way about Tony. It was no wonder. Even to his kid sister he seemed a glamorous sort of guy.

Rette said, "All right, I'll take it," because she felt helpless to make a wiser choice. She drew three limp dollar bills from her wallet, asked to have the book wrapped as a gift, and waited impatiently for the parcel and her change.

All the way home, with her head tucked down against the smarting wind, Rette worried about her purchase. She had wanted to choose a gift that would be distinctively hers, and what did she have? A book that she'd never read, that she had heard of only vaguely, that belonged more to the dark-haired girl than to anyone else, that wasn't her present at all.

In front of the house a Buick was parked, and the family Chevy was in the garage. Rette knew before she opened the storm door that her mother had guests, and that Mrs. Wynn was among them. She wished she could avoid greeting everyone by going around the back way, but her mother's friends would be sure to hear her, and it would only make her look odd. She heaved a sigh and prepared a smile as she pulled off her mittens and tugged at the scarf that bound her short brown hair.

"Rette!" Mrs. Larkin called as the house door creaked behind her daughter. "You must be frozen!" She paused in pouring a cup of tea, twisting her head so that she could see into the hall.

"Will you have some tea, dear?"

"No, thanks."

Rette dropped her mittens and the book on the Victorian sofa. Her nose felt big and pink and icy, and she knew that her hair was mashed flat by the scarf. "It's the wind," she said shortly, and had to rub her stiff fingers together before she unbuttoned her coat.

Mrs. Larkin stretched forth a slender arm, encased in striped wool jersey. "Well, darling," she said brightly, "won't you come and say hello to my guests? You've met Mrs. Edmond and Mrs. Webster, and of course you know Mrs. Wynn."

Rette read into her mother's words the implication that she had been tardy. The eyes of the women seemed pene-

4

trating as she crossed the room, and she tried to fluff up her short hair that had lost its curl in the dry cold.

"Good afternoon," she managed, with an inflection that was almost sulky. Older women always made her feel ill at ease. They seemed so utterly complacent and assured.

Actually, Rette envied this assurance. Of them all, she secretly envied her mother most. She was so debonair, so chic, so effortlessly easy and gracious. She never seemed to feel tied up inside, as Rette so frequently did. She never seemed to say the wrong thing.

Mrs. Wynn put down her teacup. "It must be getting late," she murmured as she nodded at Rette. "Did you walk home with Elise, by any chance?"

"No, I didn't." Again Loretta spoke with a shortness that sounded rude, even to her own ears. She never walked home with Elise Wynn, although they lived within two blocks of each other, and it seemed to her that Mrs. Wynn must certainly know this. Elise was one of the most popular girls in the senior class and she usually walked home with a boy.

Mrs. Webster helped herself to a water-cress sandwich and settled back comfortably. "Elise is getting to look more like you every day," she told Mrs. Wynn.

"Why, thank you!" Flattered, Mrs. Wynn raised her chin jauntily and smiled.

"She's such a pretty child," added Mrs. Larkin, and Rette could feel her own smile freeze.

"I'll bet she has lots of beaux," Mrs. Edmond commented.

"She has," chuckled Elise's mother. "She gets into some pretty funny entanglements once in a while."

Uneasily, Rette shifted feet. The women's conversation had excluded her, but she couldn't find a way to get out of the room. "Well, I guess I'd better go see Gramp," she muttered after a minute. Feeling awkward and increasingly unattractive, she gathered up her outdoor things and Tony's present and hurried up the stairs.

"Lark?"

Gramp's wheezy old voice called the pet name the moment Rette reached the second floor.

"Hi!" Rette called back. "I'll be right there." But she stood in the hall for a minute, perfectly quiet, long enough to hear her mother's voice say lightly: "They're so very 'teen' at this stage, aren't they? Rette sleepwalks around the house with her eyes wide open. I often wonder what she's thinking about."

Rette bit her lip. Apologizing for her indirectly, that's what her mother was doing. Trying to bridge the contrast between her own daughter and Elise Wynn. So certainly did she believe this that Rette's cheeks burned.

"Lark!"

"Coming!" Loretta dropped her things on her own bed and went into the south bedroom, where a thin old man was sitting in the curve of a bay window. His blue eyes, though a little rheumy, were as bright as buttons, and the welcoming smile that broke over his face when he saw his granddaughter was as spontaneous as a boy's.

"Gad, it's been a long day. Come here!"

Rette ran across the room and put her cold, red cheek against Gramp's. His skin had the dry feel of parchment, and he smelled pleasantly of Florida water. "Why particularly long?" she asked.

"Your mother's been entertaining those women," the old man complained. "Gabble-gabble-gabble all afternoon."

"Sh!" Rette giggled. "They'll hear you. This is a small house."

"Too small," Gramp agreed. "I feel cooped up." He wriggled a little, and Rette knew he was remembering the big rooms and high ceilings of his old house on King Street.

6

"You're just a chronic complainer," she scolded, though she knew he wasn't. She grinned to show she was teasing and gently pinched the lobe of her grandfather's ear.

He put his hand over hers and pulled it down. "Now that you're home," he said, "it's all right. That chitter-chatter was just getting on my nerves." His free hand moved to a two-drawer stand at his side. "Time for a little pinochle, Sis?"

Rette was expecting the question. "I guess so. Until Mother wants me to help with dinner, anyway." She moved a small table between them, feeling more relaxed than she had all afternoon.

Gramp shuffled, his stiff fingers still expert. "Your grandmother," he chortled as though it were a private job, "always contended life was too short to waste on cards."

"It is," said Rette.

"Eh?" Gramp's eyes met hers sharply. "Nonsense. You cut."

Rette grinned at him and tapped the cards. Gramp dealt, and they played until the short February twilight deepened into night. Rette didn't win a game, though she used all her skill. His success tickled Gramp and he teased her. "Eighty my next birthday, and you just sixteen!"

Loretta's chin came up, but she didn't reply.

Gramp leaned back in his chair. " 'Sweet sixteen and never been kissed,' " he added with the inevitability of night following day.

Rette recognized it for the feeble humor of the aged and knew there was no reason to resent it. Yet she could feel a flush creeping from her neck to her cheeks, and she had to keep her back turned to Gramp as she put the cards into their box. She wished people could just let her alone!

Downstairs, Mrs. Larkin was saying good-by to Mrs. Edmond, the last of her guests. In the midst of the flurry of leave-taking Rette could hear the telephone ring, so she went to Gramp's door and called, "I'll get it," then lifted the receiver from the extension in the upstairs hall.

"Mum?"

It was Tony's voice, brisk and light.

"No. This is Rette." It always surprised Loretta that on the phone even members of the family could mistake her for her mother. "D'you want Mother? I can call her."

"Never mind. Just tell her I won't be home for dinner—probably not until quite late."

"Oh!" Rette said. "Oh, all right."

There was a flatness to her voice that carried over the wire. Ready to hang up, Tony hesitated. "Nothing's wrong, is there?"

"No. Nothing's wrong."

"O.K. then, Small Fry. I'll be seein' you."

"O.K.," Rette repeated. " 'By."

She stood with her hand still on the receiver after she had replaced it. When Tony didn't come home for dinner it made the family seem incomplete; it brought back some of the feeling of the war years. Yet, of course, there was no reason why Tony shouldn't stay out tonight or any other night he chose. Rette shrugged off her momentary disappointment and clattered downstairs.

Her mother was already washing up the tea things and thinking about dinner.

"Thanks for playing with Gramp awhile, darling," she said to Rette with a smile. "I could tell from the way he was stamping around that we were getting on his nerves."

"That's all right." Idly, Rette picked up a dish towel and started drying the cups and saucers. Then she wished she hadn't, because her mother's next remark was a question.

"Why don't you like Elise Wynn?"

"I like her. I never said I didn't, did I?" Rette made her reply a challenge, to divert her mother and prevent her from recognizing that the shoe was on the other foot.

Rette's pride kept her from acknowledging that it was Elise who ignored her. Elise was too busy and too pre-occupied to bother much with girls whose interests she didn't understand or share.

"She seems like such an attractive girl," Mrs. Larkin mused as she turned from the sink to start to peel pota-toes.

"She is."

"She has a great deal of poise for her age."

"Yep," Rette admitted.

Mrs. Larkin frowned. "I wish you wouldn't say, 'yep.'"

"O.K."

"Or 'O.K.' either." Mrs. Larkin sighed, then chuckled. "Look, darling, you're growing up. I know it sounds stuffy to say that some words are—" she waved a paring knife— "are unladylike, but they are."

"And suppose I don't especially want to be a lady?" Rette's eyes were stormy as they met her mother's. Sud-denly, without any warning, she threw down the dish towel and ran out of the room.

9

CHAPTER TWO

Afterward, of course, Rette was ashamed. She hated scenes, and she knew her mother hadn't meant to be hypercritical or unkind. Yet she couldn't bring herself to apologize in words. She made amends in another way—by setting the table for dinner without being asked.

As she put on the place mats, the silver, the bread-and-butter plates, she berated herself. Why she was subject to these black moods when she turned sullen or silent, she didn't quite understand. Except that she felt, in the past year or so, that people had been trying to make her over. Her mother, most of all.

Rette really adored her mother. That was why any criticism from her cut deep. Mrs. Larkin was so feminine, so popular, so completely jelled as a person, that she made Rette feel more than ever unformed.

She had inherited none of her mother's physical characteristics except her wide-set gray-blue eyes and her husky voice, which contributed to the reputation Rette had acquired as a child of being the "tomboy" type.

"The tomboy type"—how Rette hated that phrase! Yet she felt compelled to continue the pose because it at least accounted for her not having dates like the other girls. It had become a shield to hide behind, and, though Rette despised herself for using it, she couldn't seem to let it drop.

"Let's have some popovers," Mrs. Larkin called in from the kitchen as Rette placed the last of the goblets. "Tony loves them. I'll whip them up if you'll butter the tins."

"Oh, I forgot to tell you! Tony called. He won't be home."

"Did he say what he was doing?"

"No, he didn't."

Rette could hear her mother chuckle. "Now if I don't sound like a biddy-hen! I've got to remember that Tony's grown up and well able to take care of himself. Let's have popovers anyway. Shall we?"

"Sure." Rette went out to the kitchen, tore off a section of paper towel from the wall rack, and started to grease the tins. "I bought Tony a birthday present today," she said after a few minutes. "A book."

"A book?"

Rette nodded and answered her mother's unspoken question. "It's called *Wind, Sand and Stars,* and it's about flying. A girl at the book shop recommended it. I hope it will be all right."

"Hope what will be all right?" A chunky, brown-haired man with a boyish sprinkling of freckles across his straight nose stood in the kitchen doorway.

"Rette," and Mrs. Larkin to her husband, "was just talking about a birthday present she bought for Tony."

Jim Larkin snapped his fingers. "Tomorrow, isn't it? I almost forgot."

"The night before Valentine's Day," murmured Rette's mother, her eyes soft. She spooned the dough into the muffin tins. "Twenty-three years—"

"What did you get for Tony, Rette?" Mr. Larkin was saying.

"A book," Loretta repeated. *"Wind, Sand and Stars."*

11

"Oh, yes!"

Obviously her father had heard of it. Rette felt reassured.

But later that evening when she took the book from its brown paper bag and carefully untied the ribbon that bound the gift wrapping, when she settled down in bed and started to turn its pages, doubt assailed her again.

It was a strange book, and it seemed to Rette to be not so much about flying as it was about a man's thoughts. Even in translation from the French, the language had a beauty and a flow that made her keep on reading, once she had started a passage. But frequently the philosophy was beyond her, and the elements about which the pilot-author was writing were entirely strange to her world.

Yet every now and again she came across a paragraph that she felt must touch closely the way Tony felt about the air.

"Flying," she read, "is a man's job and its worries are a man's worries. A pilot's business is with the wind, with the stars, with night, with sand, with the sea. He strives to outwit the forces of nature. He stares in expectancy for the coming of dawn the way a gardener awaits the coming of spring. He looks forward to port as to a promised land, and truth for him is what lives in the stars."[*]

"Flying is a man's job," Rette read again, and lay back on the pillow. When she read sentences like this she wished, almost desperately, that she had been born a boy. It seemed to her that a man's life was so much more direct than a woman's. You simply chose a goal and worked toward it, and there with nothing, given youth and strength, that couldn't be achieved. You didn't have to be glamorous or charming or even particularly attractive. You weren't caught in a web of artificialities, like a girl.

[*] Reprinted from Antoine de Saint-Exupéry's *Wind, Sand and Stars*, Reynal & Hitchcock, Inc., N. Y.

"Rette, better put your light out. Tomorrow's a school day."

How many times had her mother said these same words, Rette wondered, as she called back, "All right." She slipped the book into a drawer of her dresser and clicked off the switch of the bedside lamp. Crawling back under the blankets, she lay flat on her stomach and thought, Well, I'm not a boy, so there's no use wishing. Then she promptly went to sleep.

She didn't waken when Tony came in, nor did she hear her alarm the next morning. Still deep in dreams when her mother touched her shoulder, Rette jerked back to consciousness abruptly.

"Better get up right away, dear. We all overslept." Even as she spoke, Mrs. Larkin turned to start downstairs.

Rette dressed automatically, with a vague feeling of alarm at the pit of her stomach that might have been caused by being startled out of sleep but that was, in more likelihood, rooted in the inescapability of a math quiz, scheduled for third-period class.

"I detest math with a vengeance," she told her assembled family at the breakfast table, but she wasn't surprised that nobody seemed disturbed.

Tony, bound for the 8:18 train to the city, was eating with one eye on the clock. Mr. Larkin was absorbed in the morning paper, and Gramp had not yet emerged from his lengthy bathroom ritual to appear downstairs. Rette's remark might have fallen into a vacuum for all the response it got.

"Tony," her mother asked from the kitchen door, "will you have one egg or two?"

"I'll skip the egg, thanks. I'm late." Tony started for the front of the house with his easy, long-legged stride. Rette could see him shrugging into his tweed topcoat, which he

13

wore open in defiance of the February winds. " 'By every-body," he called from the doorway. "See you tonight."

"For dinner?" Mrs. Larkin asked.

"Sure thing." Tony grinned back at his mother and was gone.

Rette returned to her hot cereal, an island in the middle of the cream. Systematically she began eating around its shore line, turning her dish as she had since she was a child. "Are we going to have a cake?" she asked.

"A cake?" Her father looked up from his newspaper.

"A cake for Tony," Mrs. Larkin interjected, putting an eggcup before Rette. "Yes, I think we should. Don't you?"

Rette nodded. "It's always more birthday-y," she said.

"Let's have a chocolate cake," proposed Mr. Larkin. He always wanted a chocolate cake, just as he always wanted a cherry pie. All other varieties he considered second-rate and scarcely worth the trouble. "How about it, Rette?"

Willingly enough, Rette nodded and became her dad's ally. She was eating too rapidly to take time to talk.

Yet in spite of her concentrated effort she too was late in getting off. "I guess I'd better take the bike," she said with a certain distaste, as she pulled on her mittens. "I'll never make it if I walk."

Covertly she glanced at her dad, who occasionally stepped up his own leave-taking enough to drop her off at school en route to his local real-estate office. But he was absorbed in his coffee and paper. He didn't even raise his head.

"I guess you'd better," Mrs. Larkin said vaguely, and settled back in her chair with a contented sigh. Rette slammed out of the house, envying both her parents their extra moments of leisure, and wheeled the despised bicycle out of the garage.

The girls in the senior class simply didn't ride bikes any more. Through a twist of fashion they had abandoned the habit six months ago as a kid practice. So as Rette pedaled, pink-nosed, through the wintry Avondale streets, she felt as conspicuous as though she were wearing Mary Janes and a smocked dress.

Consequently, in response to an occasional, "Hi, Rette!" from a hurrying classmate, she was almost curt. She wanted to get her bicycle parked as soon as possible, and it was with considerable relief that she reached her home-room desk.

The assembly bell had not yet rung, and there was the usual preschool shuffle and chitchat. Corky Adams, a thin boy with glasses who sat directly behind her, lowered a copy of the *Avondale Blade*, the town's slender weekly, the moment Loretta dropped her books on her desk.

"Say, Rette."

Loretta turned, rather surprised. Corky rarely attempted to be social.

The boy folded the newspaper back to page one and handed it to her, pointing to an item at the top. "I bet your brother'll be interested in this."

Rette's expression softened. As a stanch admirer of Tony's, Corky couldn't help having some virtue in her eyes. She read the headline obediently.

WINGS AIRPORT TO OPEN
ON SITE OF FORMER
TISDALE FARM

"I know," she said. "Isn't that exciting?"

Corky blinked up at her. "Will Tony fly there, d'you expect?"

Rette shook her head. "I doubt it. He flies once a week with the Reserve, and that's about all he has time for."

Corky looked disappointed. "That's too bad. With a field so close to where you live—"

Rette thought it was too bad too, but she took a more mature view of the situation than Corky. "Anyway," she said, "flying's pretty expensive, and Tony's just getting started in a new business. He might not be able to afford it, even if he did have the time."

"What business is he in?" Corky changed the conversation but not the subject.

"He sells for an oil company. Not at a gas station," Rette explained, "but to something called 'commercial users.' I don't quite understand what that means."

"I do," Corky nodded knowingly. "Selling," he said in a statement that sounded like a direct quotation from his father, "is a great game if you've got the temperament."

He looked so much like a wise little owl that Rette could hardly stifle a giggle. "I guess."

She turned back to her own desk just as a tall girl, looking very efficient, came down the aisle toward her.

"O Loretta," she said, consulting a list she carried, "Miss Corwin wanted me to tell you. You're starting in the Claremont game."

Rette nodded, unaware of the envious glance of Margaret Lewis, who sat across the aisle. She had played varsity basketball since she was a sophomore. Like Tony, she possessed a certain natural co-ordination that made her good at most sports. It had never occurred to her that this was a thing to be cherished. Success, by her own count, was quite a different thing.

She would have felt successful if she could have walked into the room smiling at Jeff Chandler, as Elise Wynn was doing just now. She followed Elise with her eyes, marveling at her apparent poise. Elise never seemed self-conscious or gawky. She had a gentleness about her, a sweet, almost kittenish quality that the boys liked.

Immediately Rette felt all elbows and knees. It was a reaction that was inevitable. Much as she struggled

16

against it, the same feeling always swept over her when Elise came near.

The assembly bell rang, and Rette rose hastily, anxious to be doing something—anything—that would provide distraction. The feeling she had about Elise was closely akin to jealousy, and Rette recognized it as a destructive emotion and fled before it down the hall to the auditorium, where she sank gratefully into a seat beside Cathy Smith.

Cathy was a comfortable sort of girl who lived in a private world composed largely of horses and dogs and demanded little of Rette or anyone else. She smiled companionably, but a little vaguely, and didn't try to make small talk. Rette wriggled a little, wound one leg around the other, and turned her attention to the platform, where the prinicpal was just appearing through the stage door, followed by a tall young man dressed in a tweed sport coat and dark-brown gabardine slacks.

There was something in the young man's bearing, something in the way he wore his clothes, something in the cut of his lean jaw and in the way his close-cropped, rebellious hair fitted his head, that made a ripple pass over the auditorium. It was a purely feminine ripple, like a prolonged "Ah," and it made the boys sit up a little straighter and take special notice of the guest. Even Cathy Smith came out of her day-dream long enough to turn to Rette and raise an appreciative eyebrow.

"Who is he, d'you know?" she asked.

Rette shook her head. "I didn't even know we were going to have a speaker," she whispered back. "That is, if he *is* a speaker."

"I hope," murmured the girl on Cathy's right.

Somehow, to Rette, the young man didn't look like a speaker. He looked as though he belonged out of doors, not on the platform of the crowded Avondale High auditorium. He had squint lines around his alert blue eyes, and his skin had a weather-tanned glow.

She waited as impatiently as the rest of the girls around her for the routine announcements to be finished, for the mechanics of the assembly program to reach the point where Mr. Martin, the principal, would explain the presence of this interesting alien.

Finally, rather ponderously, Mr. Martin came to the point. "I want to introduce Mr. Stephen Irish," he said, "who is connected with Avondale's maiden venture in aviation. Mr. Irish has a proposal to make that may be of interest to some of the upperclassmen—especially the boys."

Mr. Martin nodded and smiled in the direction of the guest speaker, and Stephen Irish came to the edge of the platform in a few strides. He scorned the lectern, behind which the principal always stood, and seemed to want to get as close as possible to his audience. Then, in a voice surprisingly brisk for its depth, he began to talk.

Rette sat entranced; he was like no assembly speaker Avondale High had ever had. As he described the inception of the new airport, and outlined its growth from dream to reality, he spoke as he might have spoken to one other person—without formality, but with a quick sincerity that made her hang on every word.

"Wings Airport is a young man's venture," he said, "and we think that our greatest and first appeal should be to youth. You people will be the civilian flyers who will make the United States the first truly air-minded country. You're going to be thinking about planes the way your grandfathers thought about cars. Did it ever occur to you that the men who drove the early cars were considered pretty venturesome boys?"

A ripple of amusement crossed the auditorium, but Rette, seeing in her imagination a picture of a bright-eyed young man trying to learn to control the first horseless carriage, was thoughtful.

Stephen Irish dug his hands into the pockets of his jacket and rocked a little on his heels. "One of you," he said, grinning, "is going to have a chance to be just as venturesome as his grandfather. One of you—probably a junior or senior—is going to have a chance to learn to fly a plane."

CHAPTER THREE

In the high-school auditorium intense quiet was followed by a stir of interest, most vocal among the older boys. Across the center aisle from where she sat, Rette could see Jeff Chandler leaning forward, his eyes on the speaker, his lips slightly parted, as though he were hanging on every word.

"Wings Airport," Mr. Irish was continuing, "is willing to give a course of flying lessons to any student sixteen years old or over who can qualify. The course will be offered as a prize in a contest, and since the details of that contest will be of interest to only a limited number of you, I suggest that Mr. Martin take over from here."

As Mr. Martin got to his feet, Rette could see the light of anticipation die in the eyes of the boys that were under sixteen. She knew how they felt; she had often experienced that sudden upsurge of excitement, followed by the dull finality of an idea's death. It made her sad to see their dream crushed. To fly—it would be such a marvelous thing! The romance of it made her spine tingle and her shoulders quiver. She glanced at Jeff Chandler again.

"The competition," Mr. Martin was saying, "will take the form of an essay contest."

Instantly a groan of disappointment could be heard from the ranks of the junior and senior boys.

The principal raised his hand. "Mimeographed forms containing contest rules will be available in the anteroom to my office," he continued. "I urge students who are interested to call for copies at once, since all entries must be submitted within one month."

He glanced at his watch, then brought the assembly to a close. Rette had a feeling that his judgment as to the wisdom of this contest was suspended. She wondered whether Mr. Martin considered flying risky and foolhardy, and rather suspected that he did.

The buzz of excitement created by Stephen Irish and his proposal increased, rather than abated, back in Rette's home room. The boys, their clannishness stimulated, gathered in little knots to talk about flying, and the girls had to exclaim over the glamorous Mr. Irish.

"If he's the instructor, I'd like to learn to fly myself!" plump Judy Carter said, with an upward roll of her eyes.

The mere idea of Judy Carter behind the controls of a plane made all the girls within hearing distance chuckle. "What's so funny about that?" Judy asked them, drawing herself erect. "I'm sixteen. I might fool you all and win the prize."

"Are girls allowed?" Elise Wynn asked.

"He didn't say they weren't."

Rette edged closer, and a pounding started in her chest —a heavy, jarring thud of excitement she couldn't control.

"Do you really think—" she began, but the sharp clap of Miss Damon's hands interrupted her.

"Will this group come to at least a semblance of order," the home-room teacher demanded in her most authoritative voice.

All through first-period French, Rette played the outgrown game of make-believe. Because she couldn't quite bring herself to hope that a girl could win the essay contest, she pretended that she was Jeff Chandler, editor of the *Avondale Arrow*, the school paper—a boy who might really stand a chance. But toward the end of the game Rette got mixed up. She carried home to Tony the marvelous news that she had won—she, Loretta Larkin—because somewhere along the way she had discarded the identity of Jeff.

Only the imminence of the algebra quiz broke into her daydreaming during second period. Rette was afraid of failure, impatient of it and afraid. Deeply rooted as the conviction was that she didn't understand math and never would, she still resented the poor grades she received. Why, when English and history and most other subjects came so easily to her, did she have to bog down in this?

A pit yawned in her stomach as she walked into the mathematics room. The questions that Mr. Scott was writing on the blackboard looked even more impossible than she had anticipated. Her shoulders sagged and she sank into her seat hopelessly. If she let her math grades fall any farther, she'd be barred from athletics in the spring.

It was hard for Rette to understand the apparent calmness with which most of her classmates attacked the problems. Judy, sitting in front of her, wrote her name in a neat, small backhand at the top of her paper and then wriggled forward with her eyes on the board. Elise, two seats to Rette's left, was already making rapid calculations on a scratch pad—proving the first problem, Rette suspected. Elise, for all her arrant femininity, was a whiz at math.

Rette fretted. She gnawed at her pencil and stared at the blackboard until it became a blur. Then, viciously, she attacked the first problem, but by the time she was halfway through she was in a hopeless muddle, so she was forced to give it up and go on to number 2. This question, and the third, weren't so bad, and Rette regained a little confidence. She sailed through a couple of questions on theory, because she had a good memory although she couldn't apply the rules she had learned. But the last five questions became increasingly difficult. All of them were problems, and three of them Rette couldn't possibly solve. She made a rapid calculation. Four out of ten questions were sure to be wrong. Unhappily, she gnawed at her pencil again and gazed around the room.

She didn't feel ashamed as much as she felt enraged. What good would math ever do her anyway? She didn't plan to be a bookkeeper or an accountant or even a teller in a bank. She wasn't interested in business—at least not in that kind of business. She began to imagine what she would like to do, after she got out of college, and she thought it would be something connected with journalism. Reporting for a newspaper, perhaps. A colorful life, an unpredictable life! It intrigued her. She put the pencil down and her eyes became dreamy.

"Having trouble, Loretta?"

Abruptly, Mr. Scott's voice cut through her thoughts. He had paused by her desk and was looking at her askance.

Rette nodded. Then, suddenly, she turned belligerent. "I'll just never be able to do math! There's no use thinking I will."

Mr. Scott smiled wisely. "You're probably quite right," he said calmly. "With that attitude, you're licked."

Rette looked up, and was alarmed by the coolness of his pale eyes. She didn't want to make things worse for herself than they already were.

"It isn't that I don't try," she murmured, then wondered if this were quite the truth. Did she study, or did she simply fume?

But Mr. Scott had passed on, and Rette had to go back to chewing her pencil. She kept her head bent over her paper and her brow knit in a frown of apparent concentration, but she didn't really see the figures that crawled in spidery disarray across the page. When she handed in the test paper it was still incomplete, and even the problems at which she had made a second attempt were obviously wrong. Eyes stormy and head indignantly high, she walked out of the room.

Once in the corridor, with the test at least behind her, Rette tried to forget the whole thing. There was no use facing bad news until it came, she reasoned, and she went down to the lunchroom to join the cafeteria line determined to think of something—anything—else.

Today that wasn't hard. The girls who weren't discussing the coming basketball game with Claremont were still discussing Stephen Irish.

"Even his name is lush!" Judy Carter said between bites of a tuna-fish sandwich. She had been well launched on her lunch before Rette put down her tray on the opposite side of the table. "And with that voice, he ought to be in Hollywood!"

Cathy Smith, sitting beside Judy, frowned. "Don't be silly, Judy. He's not the movie type at all. He's too—too masculine."

Rette knew that Cathy wasn't saying quite what she meant. Cathy sensed the flyer's affinity with the out of doors, and it offended her to hear him wrongly categorized. Rette listened to the argument that followed with interest, but didn't try to take part. After Judy's final shrug she changed the subject.

"Has anybody seen a copy of the contest rules?"

"I have," Judy said at once. "I stopped in and picked one up, just for fun. But I haven't got it here. I left it with my books."

Rette was disappointed. "What was it all about?"

"Like Mr. Irish said. An essay of a thousand words. Gosh, a thousand words sound like a lot!"

"Not too bad," Rette said. As make-up editor for the *Arrow* she had counted a good many words. "That's about four pages, typewritten, double-spaced."

Cathy, looking misty-eyed again, was paying no attention to the conversation. Rette half envied her her detachment. It must, she thought, be rather pleasant to just sit back and let the world flow around you like water in a bathtub. Wanting to be part of things so much got rather wearing.

Just now Rette wanted to know the subject of the essay, but at the same time she didn't want to sound *too* interested in the contest. The last thing she cared to invite was an inquiry from Judy as to whether she planned to take part. She wished Cathy would rouse and ask the question for her, but Cathy was a million miles away.

Finally her curiosity became too great. "What do you have to write about—airplanes?" Rette asked. Her voice, always deep, sounded unnaturally loud in her own ears. It fell into one of those inexplicable pools of quiet that suddenly emerge in a noisy room. It was as though Rette were the only person left talking, and her voice boomed forth with such vigor that Elise Wynn and her crowd, who were eating at the next table, all turned their heads.

"You thinking of getting into competition with the boys, Rette?" A pretty girl with straight bangs above slanting dark eyes leaned back in her chair and spoke over her shoulder idly.

Rette flushed, disliking the insinuation. "I was just interested," she muttered lamely. "Is there anything wrong with that?"

"I'm interested too." Elise Wynn unexpectedly came to her rescue. "What is the subject, Judy? Do you know?"

Judy nodded, swinging around in her chair. "It's sort of peculiar—'The Dream of Flying.'" Her eyes met Elise's. "Can you make anything of that?"

25

" 'The Dream of Flying,' " Elise repeated, as though she were tasting the words with the tip of her tongue. She paused, then smiled. "Well, I'd say it would give people a lot of scope."

"The Dream of Flying." Rette didn't say the words aloud but they spoke in her brain. They sounded evanescent, impossible to capture. She had expected to hear a more concrete title. She wondered who had thought this subject up.

Abruptly, she said as much.

"Not Mr. Irish, I'll bet," Judy replied.

"I don't know," Cathy murmured; "he might have." It didn't seem to occur to her that she was contradicting Judy again.

This time, to Rette's relief, Judy had her mouth too full of apple pie to reply immediately, and by the time she was vocal the conversation had swept onward, because the girls at Elise Wynn's table were making a game of guessing which of the senior boys might compete.

"Jeff Chandler will, of course. He's nuts about planes," Dora Phillips said.

"And besides," seconded the girl next to her, "he can write."

"Dick Sharp, Larry Carpenter, John Hall—you can practically count them on your fingers. I'll bet there won't be more than a dozen entries in all."

"I think Dora's wrong," Rette said in an undertone to Judy. "I think some of the kids who are Corky Adams' type will take a shot at turning in a paper."

"Corky?"

Rette nodded. "He was all steamed up about the new airport, even before Mr. Irish spoke."

"But—" Judy stopped, shrugged, and shook her head.

"I could be wrong," Rette said, but she didn't sound convinced.

26

On the way back to her home room after lunch, Rette passed the principal's office. Larry Carpenter and John Hall were just coming out, openly studying copies of the contest rules. Rette could hear John's complaining whistle as they turned and came along the corridor behind her.

"Hey, this is a heck of a subject!"

She wished she had the courage to turn around to go into the anteroom for her own copy. She wasn't usually timid, but she didn't want people asking questions about her intentions. Especially since she didn't really have any intentions; she was just curious. It would be foolish, she supposed, for any girl to have a serious hope of winning the prize when the natural candidate was a boy. Yet all afternoon, even during the warming-up period before the Claremont game, the thought of the contest continued to tempt her. Only when the referee's whistle actually blew and the Claremont forward dodged past her to catch a quick pass from side-center did Rette snap back to complete attention to the business at hand.

CHAPTER FOUR

"... Who are we for?
Larkin! Larkin!
Rah, rah, rah!"

Applause fell sweetly on Rette's ears during the third quarter of the Claremont game. The balcony of the gym was full, with a generous sprinkling of boys among the girls who usually turned out to root for the Avondale team.

Rette was playing unusually well, and she knew it. The Claremont forwards were swift and tall, but not many unguarded balls had slipped through the basket, and at the half the score totaled in Avondale's favor, which sent the refreshed team back to the court foretasting victory.

It would be quite a feather in the school's cap to beat Claremont. And it was a personal triumph for Rette that a guard, not a forward, was being cheered. She felt the elation of success, and played all the better. She was glad the Claremont forwards were outstanding. It made the competition keener, more fun.

Rette was small, for a guard, but she was lightning-quick. She clung to the Claremont forward with the tenacity of a terrier.. Here, there, everywhere at once, she was impossible to shake.

28

By the fourth quarter Avondale's lead was substantial, and the coach began putting in second-string players to replace the stars. Rette walked back to the players' bench reluctantly when a substitute guard came forward. Far from exhausted, she felt that she could play forever. The stimulation of the game made her eyes shine, and her short hair curled in damp tendrils around her face.

The same sense of stimulation accompanied her all the way home. Dusk was blurring the harsh outlines of winter when Rette left the gym, and under its cover she could ride her bicycle the scant mile to Cherry Tree Road without special concern for whom she might meet. She hummed as she wheeled along, standing on the pedals to increase her speed, still imbued with a feeling of power and of glowing well-being.

"We beat Claremont!" she announced the minute she reached the house.

"Good for you!" her mother sang out from the kitchen. "Tell Gramp. He'll be pleased."

"Beat 'em?" Rette's grandfather was already asking, as he came shakily down the stairs with one gnarled, thin hand clutching the banister. "Beat 'em, Rette? Yep? That's fine!"

Gramp always exulted with Rette in her victories, always sympathized with her in defeat. She could have no more loyal and interested supporter, and she knew it. "Tell me all about it," he insisted, lowering himself with the care of age into the chintz-covered wing chair.

Rette ran to him, laughing, and laid her smooth red cheek against his forehead. "Don't rush me," she teased, wrinkling her nose. "Wait till I get off my coat."

"And while you're giving Gramp a play-by-play description would you like to lay a fire?" Mrs. Larkin said from the doorway. "We're having Tony's birthday dinner tonight, you know."

"With presents at the table the way we used to when you were young?" Gramp asked hopefully.

Mrs. Larkin nodded. "Yes, indeed."

Gramp sighed reminiscently, and Rette could see his interest in the game fading. "I remember when Nancy was just about your age," he said, looking after his daughter. "She was going to a party on the night of her birthday, and her beau sent her a box of flowers from the florist. What is it you call it now—a corsage? I'll never forget the look in her eyes." He hesitated a moment, then said thoughtfully, "I wonder if that could have been George?"

Rette laughed. "Probably not," she said as she wadded newspaper to tuck under the kindling. "You've always said Mother had lots of beaux!"

"She did too!" Gramp insisted proudly. "A mighty pretty girl, your mother was." He looked at Rette and added in a shrewd stage whisper, "But no sweeter than you."

"I've got to wrap Tony's present," Rette cried, jumping up. "I'll tell you about the game after dinner, Gramp. All right?"

Gramp nodded. "I guess it'll keep." He called after her, "Get the box that's on my bureau, Rette, while you're upstairs."

By six o'clock everything was ready. The chocolate cake, nesting in a fluff of white icing, reposed on the kitchen cabinet. A small heap of boxes lay on Tony's place mat, Rette's book, the bulkiest, at the bottom. New candles graced the low candelabra, and hothouse snapdragons, testimony to the fact that this was a party, were arranged with tasteful frugality in a low white bowl.

Rette, upstairs, was running a comb through her hair when Tony and her dad came into the house together. She could hear Tony's approving comment when he spotted the cake.

"Boy, Mommy, that looks good enough to eat!"

Rette smiled to herself, amused by his use of "Mommy." When Tony was extra pleased about something, the old, boyish appellation always slipped out.

She dusted her short nose with powder, searched in vain for her only lipstick, then bit at her lips to redden them and clattered blithely downstairs.

"Hi!" she called from the landing. "I'm glad it's your birthday, Tony. We're going to have a real feed!"

"Rette!" Her mother pretended to be provoked at such slang.

Tony sniffed. "I saw the cake. What else?"

"Roast beef." Rette told him nothing his nose couldn't discover. "Boy, do you rate!"

"Try going away for a couple of years. You'll rate too." Tony grinned up the stairway at Rette, then winked slyly.

"Quiet!" his mother called as he had anticipated. "Rette will be off to college soon enough."

"Too soon," said Gramp from the depths of his chair.

"Much too soon," agreed George Larkin, tossing his hat and gloves to the closet shelf beside Tony's. "I'm the guy that's got to put up the dough."

"Such language!" his wife scolded. "How do you ever expect me to persuade Rette to speak properly?" She stood in the doorway, hands on her hips, and shook her head.

Rette chuckled, ducked away from her father's attempt to rumple her hair, and went over to the fireplace to touch a match to her carefully constructed fire. She loved the family badinage, which always seemed especially bright when they were all together on such special occasions as this. She was glad there were no guests for dinner, because now there could be no possible cause for strain. She liked home best when everyone felt agreeable and relaxed.

31

Tony, when he saw the roast beef, elected to save the opening of his gifts until the dessert course. "There were times in the Army," he said, "when I used to dream about roast beef. It would get so I could smell it." His grin became sardonic. "That always woke me up."

Gramp sat, straight-backed, on his chair. "I used to dream about it too, right here at home," he said, and everybody laughed.

Rette had a second helping, and so did Tony. Gramp refused and had to be coaxed. "You know you want it," Rette told him. "Or are you afraid of getting fat?"

Finally the cake was cut, and Rette's father, with unexpected ebullience, led off in singing the old nursery song,

"Happy birthday to To-ny,
Happy birthday to you!"

Everybody joined in, Mrs. Larkin with a sweet contralto, Rette tunelessly but with enthusiasm.

Gramp capped their efforts by wheezing: "Stand up! Stand up!" until Tony arose and with mock seriousness took a bow.

"And now you'd better open your presents," Gramp said.

Rette sat smiling while the old man hovered over the presents, pleased to be part of the festivity, childlike in his desire to get to the climax of the celebration. She loved Gramp with a tenderness that was occasionally overwhelming, but it never failed to alarm her to see how people can revert—growing bigger and bigger in mind and stature until maturity and then shriveling up and becoming quite simple and childish again in age.

Tony fell in with Gramp's game and obligingly rattled the small box on top close to his ear.

"Can you guess, Gramp?"

Rette sat back and watched her brother, intensely proud of him. Tony was such a marvelous sport, to indulge an old man's whimsey this way. She watched his eyes, gray-blue like her mother's and compassionate, and an indefinable emotion made her throat ache. No boy she had ever met could compete with Tony! He had everything—masculinity, courage, deftness—and then this quick, understanding courtesy that brought the smart of tears to her eyes.

Gramp was in seventh heaven. He rattled the box too and pretended to guess, but deliberately guessed wrong. Then Tony untied the cord and opened the package to draw out a wallet of polished reptile.

"Say now!" He ran his fingers over it. "That's the stuff!" He read the card. " 'Mother and Dad.' " Then he looked up with sincere pleasure. "Gee, thanks."

"Just what I needed," mimicked Rette, to inject a note of foolishness and avert any threatened sentimentality.

Tony looked at her with assumed sternness. "It is."

Next he opened a tie from a thoughtful relative, and then Gramp impatiently handed him the box Rette had brought down from his bureau. Tony made a special ceremony of the unwrapping, and Gramp stood by almost as full of pleasure as he was of years.

It was another tie, blue and gray—not a pattern that Tony would have chosen to wear with his youthful, tweedy clothes. Rette knew at once that it was all wrong, but never by a flicker of an eyelash did Tony admit it. His enthusiasm sounded utterly genuine, and his thanks warmed Gramp as he went back to sit down in his chair beside Rette. The old man smiled at his granddaughter happily, and she smiled back at him.

Then Rette's attention returned to Tony. He was opening the last package now, her book. She waited anxiously, because she'd know whether Tony was pleased. He couldn't fool her.

He laid back the paper and read the title aloud. "*Wind, Sand and Stars.*" Then he opened the book to the flyleaf, where Rette had tucked a card.

"Say, this is the book by that flyer—" He looked at his younger sister and tested his pronunciation of the name. "Saint-Exupéry. Didn't he lose a leg in the war?"

Rette shook her head. "I don't know." Then she added, "Tell me if you've read it."

"I haven't. I'd like to." Tony riffled the pages and paused at a chapter heading. "It's supposed to be quite a book."

"The girl in the bookstore said it was sort of special. I didn't know what to get—" Suddenly Rette found herself spilling over with words, with the things she had meant not to say. But Tony looked up, interested. "What girl in what bookstore?"

"Downtown. She said she knew you."

"All the girls know Tony," Mr. Larkin teased.

"What was her name?" Tony asked, unperturbed.

"I don't know. She was dark, and looked as if she maybe ought to still be in college." Rette wished she hadn't dragged the book clerk into this.

"Pretty?"

"I guess so." Rette wriggled. "She said she didn't know you very well."

Tony snapped his fingers, remembering. "Ellen Alden, I'll bet. I ought to look her up some time. She's a nice gal."

Rette didn't meet Tony's eyes. She stared at her plate. "I'd like another piece of cake, please," she said to her mother to change the subject. But when she began to eat it, the cake felt dry in her mouth. She was annoyed at the bookstore girl for walking in on Tony's birthday dinner, even though she had introduced her herself.

34

Because Rette was normally so brusque and casual, Tony was unaware that she felt let down. He continued to turn the pages of the book with interest for a few minutes, then slapped it shut and ran his hand over the jacket. "Thanks, Small Fry. This is swell."

Rette grunted an acknowledgment, glanced up and realized that her mother was aware of her discomposure. Embarrassed, she began talking again quickly. "You know the new airport they're opening out on the Tisdale place —one of the men in charge there spoke at assembly today."

Both her father and Tony gave her their attention, but Gramp was slumped in an after-dinner doze.

"His name was Stephen Irish," Rette hurried on. "Do you know him, Tony?"

Tony hesitated, but his dad prodded his flagging memory. "You know him and so do I. One of the boys in that big family out Mill Creek way. He was ahead of you in high school, Tony. Good-looking kid with a lot of drive. I think he flew a bomber in the war."

Tony's eyes narrowed thoughtfully. "Seems to me I know who you mean. Look as Irish as his name?"

Rette nodded, amused at his description. "He has the Irish gift of gab too. He really sold that airport to the kids."

Tony looked curious. "What was the idea?"

"The airport is sponsoring an essay contest, of all things," Rette told her family. "The prize is pretty special —a course of flying lessons. Isn't that something?"

Tony caught his father's eye in a man-to-man glance. "Must be a publicity-minded crowd."

"Tackling the youngsters who'll be their future stock in trade," agreed Mr. Larkin. "I suppose the older boys got all steamed up?"

Rette nodded, then said hesitatingly, "I think girls can get in on it too."

"Heavens! I pity young Irish!" groaned her dad.

Mrs. Larkin sprang to the defense of her sex. "I don't see why you say that, George. Some women make very fine pilots. Look at all those ferry-command flyers during the war!"

The men both laughed, and Nancy Larkin bridled. "Well!"

Tony, sitting next to her, squeezed his mother's arm affectionately, "You'd have made a cute little suffragette. Wouldn't she, Dad?"

George Larkin raised a militant fist. "Women's rights!"

His wife took the teasing good-naturedly, but nevertheless she turned to Rette for support. "Well, I just wish a girl would win the prize," she said with a grin. "That would show them!"

Gramp woke up. "Show them what?" he asked, afraid of missing something.

"Show the men that women have got to be reckoned with," explained his daughter.

Gramp's head dropped again. He mumbled, "That's not news."

Rette laughed aloud, precipitately swept upward by the same sense of stimulation she had felt after the Claremont game. She pushed back her chair and dug her hands into the pockets of her jumper.

"The subject of the essay's sort of hard to make out. It's 'The Dream of Flying,'" she said.

CHAPTER FIVE

Later that evening, Rette sat cross-legged on the hooked rug in front of her bedroom window seat. Surrounded by stacks of clippings, she was turning the pages of a big scrapbook when Tony, in pajamas and a maroon wool robe, wandered in.

"For this time of night," he said, "you look busy."

Loretta glanced up. "I wish I'd pasted up all this stuff as I went along," she said. "Now it's mixed up and I forget."

"What stuff?" Tony crouched and picked up a clipping.

"The things that were printed about the 82d. I kept a scrapbook. Don't you remember? I showed it to you."

"Of course, I remember now." Tony's rejoinder was a little too quick to be convincing. "That was a swell thing for you to do."

"There isn't much about flying, anyway," Rette said. "I'd sort of hoped there was."

Tony looked incredulous. "Not much about flying? In clippings about the 82d Airborne?"

"I mean small-plane flying. Oh, there's lots about paratroopers and gliders and stuff!"

Tony picked up another clipping. "You really followed the boys, didn't you, Rette? For a kid, that's kind of amazing. From Casablanca to Berlin."

"That's what I ought to call my scrapbook," Rette said. "From Casablanca to Berlin."

Tony rocked back on his heels, his arms crossed on his knees. "It was a long haul," he said. "Not many of 'em made it." Then, as though he suddenly realized what he was saying and regretted it, he stood up. "There's a book out called the *Saga of the All American*. It tells the story of the Division in pictures. Someday I ought to look it up."

"You ought to buy a copy," Rette said firmly. Her eyes twinkled and she added, "For your grandchildren." She started to gather up the little piles of newspaper clippings, which were already growing brittle and yellow. "My scrapbook will have turned to dust by then."

Tony ruffled Rette's hair gently, the way her dad often did. "I wish I could have been a paratrooper for you, Baby. They were the real glamour guys of our war."

Rette's chin lifted defensively. "I don't think so at all. I think you liaison pilots did the most important job. After all, if it hadn't been for you—"

But Tony cut her off with a laugh. "Family loyalty's a fine thing, but don't overdo it," he cautioned over his shoulder as he sauntered out of the room.

Packing the rest of the clippings away, Rette came across a picture of a tiny Cub, the type of plane Tony had flown for the artillery. It looked scarcely bigger than a bird, photographed as it was with a long-range lens. She wondered how it felt to pilot a plane like that.

Rette had flown just once, when she and her mother and dad had gone by United Air Lines to New York to meet Tony on his return from overseas. The big, four-motored plane had seemed impressive and powerful, but it was hard for Rette to think of it in the same terms as one of the light trainers that had taxied around the outskirts of each airfield like a flock of day-old chicks around a big mother hen.

She wished she could get inside Tony's mind, could know how he felt about flying. It was a subject on which he seemed utterly inarticulate—or perhaps, Rette thought, he was simply disinclined to discuss anything connected with the war. That could be the answer.

She put the scrapbook back into the long drawer under the window seat and undressed slowly, trying to imagine what it would be like actually to sit behind the controls of a plane. She wondered whether she'd be scared. She didn't think so. She planned what she would wear—slacks and a short coat. Then, with a shake of her shoulders, she mumbled, "I'm certainly putting the cart before the horse." But after she was in bed, with the down quilt pulled high under her chin, she kept on dreaming—dreaming "with her eyes wide open"—just as her mother had said.

So self-absorbed was she that Rette forgot, until she walked into her home room at school the next morning, that the date on the calendar had been turned to February 14. A single white envelope lay on the top of her desk, but two aisles away Elise Wynn was exclaiming over a pile of assorted missives.

"I think valentines are silly, at our age," Rette said to Margaret Lewis as she dropped into her seat. "Don't you?"

Margaret, much as she admired Rette's athletic ability, refused to be bulldozed. "Oh, I don't know," she said. "I think they're sort of fun."

Rette snorted, and glanced again toward Elise, around whose desk several of her friends were gathering. "Kid stuff," Rette said.

Yet curiosity made her open the sealed white envelope on her own desk before the assembly bell rang. Occasionally—and, Rette felt, absurdly—there surged in her heart the hope that she might have an unknown admirer. She secretly cherished the outside chance that someone—someone unidentifiable but very masculine—might think the boyish type of girl was appealing.

But not today.

The valentine, a cutout of a girl with a basketball, was initialed quite openly "M.L." It was from Margaret, of course—simply a friendly gesture. Rette could have bitten her tongue for what she had just said.

Sheepishly she glanced at the girl across the aisle. "Golly, thanks. I'm sorry—"

Margaret waved her hand in a gesture of negation. "Skip it."

"I pull the most awful boners." Rette tried to laugh at herself.

"We all do," Margaret said. "I know how you feel about the valentines. It's just one of those things."

Rette let it go at that, but Margaret didn't really know how she felt, Rette thought, as she went to assembly. Margaret didn't know that actually she was envious of Elise, that her scorn grew out of disappointment. It was something that, except when she was in a mood for self-castigation, she refused even to admit to herself. Usually she sought to convince herself that she was just different, that the interest most of the girls showed in boys was silly, or that actually she was a little superior to the common clay.

But none of it was true. In her heart Rette knew that she was only making one excuse after another for a lack she felt deeply. Surreptitiously she watched the popular girls when they talked to boys. How were they different from her, she wondered? What did they *do*?

Actually to Rette, they often seemed self-conscious and coy. She didn't think their antics were too attractive, but the boys seemed to like them, and she would have been glad to copy their technique if only she could.

But somehow Rette always missed the cue. She either talked too earnestly, or laughed too boisterously, or she became tongue-tied in the presence of a lone boy and couldn't talk at all. Lately, she had given up her unsuccessful experiments and adopted a swaggering, I-don't-care attitude, trying her level best to dismiss the entire subject of the opposite sex from her mind.

Of course she might as well have tried to stop the sun from shining. Boys, like death and taxes, were in Avondale to stay. Rette met them at every turn of the high-school corridor. She sat beside them in classes. She rubbed elbows with them in the lunchroom.

She even bumped smacked into Jeff Chandler as she turned into the principal's anteroom, having finally gathered courage, during assembly, to stop in for her own copy of the contest rules.

"Whoa!" Jeff backed off like a wary prize fighter.

"I'm sorry." Rette plunged past him, too embarrassed to apologize with a smile.

She grabbed a sheet from the diminishing stack of mimeographed forms and turned to go out. Jeff was standing just where she had left him, reading the rules.

He glanced up. "You aimin' to sign your name to an essay, Rette?"

Rette ducked her head and shrugged. "I just thought I'd like to see what it was all about."

"It's a toughie," Jeff said. "But, boy, would it be worth working for! That's some prize."

"It is," Rette agreed. "Why don't you get busy and win it?"

Jeff's glance was level. "You're good in English. Why don't you?"

Rette laughed shortly. "I don't honestly think a girl will stand a chance."

"I don't see why not," Jeff replied. "It's a free country." He let Loretta go out of the door in front of him. "Elise

41

Wynn and Judy Carter both claim they're going to give it a whirl."

"Elise?" Astonishment was written on Rette's face. She knew Judy was apt to tackle anything in a spirit of good-natured playfulness, but Elise—?

"Why not?"

"I'm just surprised," Rette admitted. "I wouldn't think Elise—"

"Would have the guts to want to learn to fly?" Jeff finished the sentence for her.

Rette didn't want to seem disparaging. "I just meant—Elise never goes in for sports much—" She hesitated, ill at ease.

Jeff grinned. "I understand flying takes brains, not brawn," he said as he left Rette at the end of the corridor. Rette walked away from him rapidly, feeling muscular and inadept.

Still, hard as she tried, she couldn't quite believe that Elise would be seriously interested in taking flying lessons. Could it be a bid for attention, Rette wondered. Was Elise simply planning to make a rather astute play to the only gallery she ever courted—the boys?

Rette knew that it was an uncharitable question to raise, so she kept it to herself. But that afternoon, when she happened to sit next to Elise in art class, she kept looking at her covertly, and she was more than ever dubious. Elise had the delicacy of a Staffordshire figurine. Even the crayon sketch she was making at the art instructor's behest was pastel and thin-lined—typical, Rette thought, of her personality. She sighed and looked down at her own robust effort in strong reds and browns, contrasting the two drawings as she had always contrasted their separate skills.

Elise glanced at Rette, then at her drawing. "That's good," she said.

Rette made a gesture of demurral. "It looks sort of slap-dash next to yours," she said honestly. Then, encouraged by Elise's overture, she brought up the subject of the contest. "Jeff Chandler was telling me you're going to submit an essay."

"Oh, I don't know." Elise seemed hesitant. "I was talking about it. But I'm not really very good at composition, you know."

This was an angle that hadn't occurred to Rette, but now that she thought about it, she realized that math, not English, was Elise's forte.

"I didn't even know you were interested in flying."

Elise picked up a blue crayon and returned to work on her drawing. "I am," she said. "I guess it's partly because of Daddy. He's been keen on it for years. And now that his plant is making airplane parts, and he's getting around to the big factories, he talks about aviation a lot. He makes it sound exciting and—well, sort of tempting. Like Mr. Irish."

Rette had met Mr. Wynn only once or twice, but she could imagine what Elise meant. He had Stephen Irish's vigor, his forthrightness, his drive. Rette knew that Mr. Wynn had the reputation of being quite successful. Elise and her mother always had lovely clothes, and Mrs. Wynn drove her own car.

Elise exchanged her blue crayon for a yellow one. "A couple of weeks ago," she continued conversationally, "Jeff was over one night and he and Daddy got started on flying." She smiled to herself, then looked up. "Jeff's the boy who really ought to win the prize."

"Why?" Rette asked.

"He'd get so much out of the flying lessons," Elise said.

The art teacher appeared at Rette's shoulder, ready to offer criticism, and then went on to Elise. Conversation was impossible for the rest of the period, although Rette would have liked to pursue the subject. She put her drawing materials away thoughtfully, deciding that Elise had showed considerable perception. Jeff Chandler always got a lot out of everything he did, from editing the *Arrow* to playing end on the varsity football team. Jeff was a versatile and intensely alive sort of boy.

Loretta walked upstairs from the basement art room slowly, then paused at the bulletin board because a crowd of seniors were gathered around it, craning her neck in idle curiosity to see what was causing the crush.

Judy, ducking out of the crowd from a position at center, told Rette the reason for the scrimmage. Everyone was signing up to go on a field trip to the airport. "With Mr. Irish the feature attraction." Judy rolled her eyes.

Rette waited around and added her name to the already long list. "A bus will leave at 3 P.M. from the main door on Monday, February 18," read the notice. "All upperclassmen desiring to attend please sign here."

"At this rate, they'll need two buses," said Corky Adams, at Rette's shoulder. "I can't understand why so many girls are going. Can you?"

Rette could, but she didn't feel called upon to enlighten him. "Corky," she said to confuse the issue further, "you're positively out of this world."

Feeling pleasantly superior, Rette turned away, but the unaccustomed feeling didn't last long. Mr. Scott, standing in the doorway of the empty math classroom, touched her on the arm.

"Could you stop in and talk with me for a few minutes after school?" he asked.

Rette's nod was full of concern. She waited for the closing bell anxiously, and then walked with reluctant feet back to see Mr. Scott. He had a paper on the desk when she arrived, and his eyes, when he held it out to her, were grave.

44

"It seems," he said without a flicker of a smile, "that you have very little fundamental conception of what this is all about."

Rette didn't have to glance at the paper to know that it was the math test, but her eyes automatically sought the grade at the top of the sheet. She might as well know the worst.

The worst was very bad indeed—a round and staring "50." Mr. Scott hadn't even bothered to dignify it with the inevitable letter E.

"If you can learn rules, you can learn to apply them," Mr. Scott said quietly. "If you want to participate in any sports this spring, Loretta, you've got to settle down to a good deal of concentrated work."

Rette wriggled internally, like an impatient filly champing at her first taste of the bit. She would have liked to bunch the paper into a little ball and fling it from her. She hated math; she always would hate math. She never in the world would be able to make figures behave!

But she didn't say any of these things. She said: "I knew I'd handed in a terrible paper. I'm sorry. I just can't seem to work out the problems. I don't really understand them, I guess."

"I guess," repeated Mr. Scott, with a movement of his upper lip that might have been a smile. "For the next month, try really applying yourself. If things don't improve, you'd better have a tutor. After all, if you're planning to go on to college, you can't just overlook a possible flunk."

Rette shook her head numbly. The word "flunk" had an ugly sound. She had always received good grades, even excellent ones, in everything but math. There was her undoing. From fractions to algebra, she had been led balking every step of the way.

Always, however, before this, she had just managed to

skin through. Now, apparently, her past was catching up with her.

"I'll be glad to work with you any Monday or Wednesday afternoon after school," Mr. Scott was saying generously. "If there's something you're having special trouble with, bring it to me then."

Something? Everything! Rette thought, but she didn't admit to such abysmal ignorance. She thanked the teacher with what grace she could muster and scooted out of the room.

CHAPTER SIX

Gramp sat beside Mrs. Larkin on the sofa, peering down at the book of snapshots that lay in her lap. Rette was seated cross-legged in front of the record cabinet, rearranging the albums so that her favorites could be more easily reached. Her dad was writing checks at the secretary, and Tony was reading "Dick Tracy." It was a typical Sunday afternoon.

"And there's Rette," Mrs. Larkin was saying, "tagging around after Tony like a fat puppy. Wasn't she a dumpling at three?"

To Gramp's old eyes the snapshot was little more than a blur, but he nodded happily. "She was a very pretty child."

"Was," repeated Rette, as though to herself.

"Here she is again," Mrs. Larkin went on, "still at Tony's heels. She used to drive him crazy—remember? Even followed him to the baseball diamond when he went off to play with the boys."

Tony looked up from the comic section. "Ask me if I remember!" he said.

Rette chuckled. "I could catch a curve by the time I was six," she said. "And I wasn't any more trouble than Scrappy Lambert's collie. He insisted on chasing every fielder."

She twisted around. "Once the boys tied both of us to the same tree."

"You didn't!" Her mother looked at Tony.

Tony nodded ruefully. "Yes, we did."

"I howled," Rette said, "and a police car came along and the cop told Tony it was against the law to tie a child to a tree in Pennsylvania."

"Now," Tony announced comfortingly, "she's beginning to make it up."

Rette didn't bother to deny it. Her shoulders shook a little with repressed laughter as she turned back to her record albums, and she said, "Would you like to hear the *Oklahoma!* music?" then didn't wait for anyone to reply.

The contagious gaiety of the songs seemed to make Tony restless. He tossed aside the paper, got up, and wandered around the living room whistling an accompaniment softly. He paused by a lamp table, picked up the copy of *Wind, Sand and Stars* Rette had given him, seemed to be about to settle down with it, then suddenly tossed it aside and went upstairs two at a time, whistling a little louder now.

Through the patter of a chorus Rette could hear him pick up the telephone and give a number, but it wasn't until the automatic changer finished its complement of records that she knew he was talking to a girl.

In this one respect, Rette decided, Tony hadn't changed since he was a leggy kid in high school and she was a child in pigtails. He still had a special telephone voice for girls. It was a habit he'd formed when he wanted, above all things, to exclude the family from his private affairs—a method of talking directly into the receiver in a tone so low that it seemed simply an indefinite rumble, with no distinguishable words.

Apparently, although it irritated the family, the girls liked it, because now, as before the war, he never seemed

48

to lack dates. Rette could hear him hang up, go whistling into his bedroom, and then the closet door and a bureau drawer banged in quick succession, which meant that he was dressing to go out.

A few minutes later Tony clattered down the stairs, pulling on a tweed sport coat as he came. He went over to the closet, stuck a hat on the back of his head, and shrugged into his topcoat. His father looked up from the telephone bill, at which he had been frowning.

"Going out?"

Tony nodded. "Need me for anything here?"

George Larkin shook his head. "Just idle curiosity," he grinned.

Tony decided to include the family in his plans. "Got a date with a girl Rette recommended," he told them. "Ellen Alden by name. She sells books."

"I never—" Rette started with a childish thrust of jealousy. But Tony was gone.

The afternoon dragged along, the midwinter gloom increasing with the hours. Rette shut the record changer and took Tony's book and went upstairs to lie on her bed.

But she didn't read. She lay and stared at the ceiling, hoping it wouldn't rain or snow to spoil the trip to the airport tomorrow, wishing Sundays weren't so long, wondering why older people always seemed to enjoy the day. After church there was nothing to do—but nothing. She supposed some of the girls, like Elise, had dates, just as Tony did. She wondered what it would be like.

Rette could count the dates she'd had during her four years in high school on the fingers of one hand. There was that awful night when Tolbert Norton had taken her to the movies. Tolbert had surprised her on the telephone, and she had acquiesced from sheer confusion, to die a thousand deaths as she walked through the summer twilight down High Street beside a boy any other girl in her crowd would have scorned.

Tolbert had pimples during that sophomore summer, but by fall he had apparently outgrown them. He'd asked Rette for just one more date, and she had turned him down haughtily. Then, to Loretta's amazement, Dora Phillips had taken him up, and Tolbert had never needed to look her way again.

There were a few other stray engagements, blind dates arranged by a friend, or boys enlisted to walk Rette to and from a party. Mostly they were unsuccessful affairs, during which Loretta, to hide her uneasiness, maintained an attitude of rather boyish camaraderie. During this last semester she had been left severely alone, and when she thought seriously about the situation, she wasn't really surprised.

Rette rolled over on her stomach and put her head in her hands, staring out at the black branches of a maple tree outlined by a street light, which was switched on at five o'clock this time of year.

She guessed she'd call Cathy Smith and see if she felt like walking over. But Cathy was absorbed in reading the last of the books in the Flicka saga and couldn't be persuaded to put it down.

There was nothing left to do but call Margaret Lewis, who made the mistake of being always available. Margaret was flattered to be asked over and came as fast as her thin legs could carry her, arriving pinched and red-nosed from the cold.

Bountifully, Rette invited Margaret to stay for a pickup supper. The girls made sandwiches while Mrs. Larkin stirred a large pot of cocoa, and they carried the food into the living room to eat in front of the open fire.

Gramp, who had retreated before "company," edged his way downstairs again and joined the family. Then he persuaded Rette to play records of some of the Gilbert and Sullivan music he loved and everyone lay back and hummed along with the expert singers from the D'Oyly Carte troupe.

Margaret, Rette could see, was captivated by her mother, as were all the girls she brought home. She was proud of her family for being vivacious and young in heart, and when Margaret praised them she said, "But your parents aren't old."

Margaret was putting on her coat and bandanna before Rette's bedroom mirror. "They're not old," she said, "but they're sort of settled. They don't understand kids very well—and they worry a lot, about money and things."

Rette laughed. "Everybody worries about money."

Margaret said, "They worry about me too."

"You?"

"About whether I'm out too late, and about my marks at school, and about—" Margaret sighed and bit her lip as though she were making a confession—"about my health." She paused, then plunged on. "For instance, they're having a fit because I want to go on that field trip to the airport tomorrow."

"But why?"

Margaret shook her head. "Flying's a lot of foolishness, and I may catch cold."

Rette laughed again, because in those few words Margaret's description of her parents was pat. "We all may 'catch our deaths,' as Gramp always says, if it doesn't warm up. Brrr."

The girls walked downstairs side by side, and Gramp rose gallantly to say good night. He took Margaret's hand and told her it had been a great pleasure to meet her. Then he eyed her cannily. "Do you play pinochle?" he asked.

"I'm afraid I don't," Margaret confessed.

51

Gramp dropped her hand immediately and turned away. "Well," he said, "well, good-by."

When Rette came back from closing the door behind her guest, he was grumbling to himself as he creaked up-stairs. "What good's all this education? Girls aren't even taught the fundamentals any more."

Rette stood with her hands on her hips, looking up at him. "Fundamentals like pinochle?" she asked.

"And can you name a better game?" he stormed back at her. Then he glanced toward the davenport, where Rette's mother was curled in a corner with her favorite magazine. "Bridge!" he snorted. It was his last word for the night.

Tony came home half an hour later, his face ruddy with cold and his gray-blue eyes sparkling. He tossed his hat and gloves on a table and came over to rub his face against the sleeve of his mother's cashmere sweater.

"I stayed for supper," he said.

Mrs. Larkin smiled. "Where there is food, there is Tony."

"You'll have to meet Ellen, Mother. She's quite a gal. Different."

"How different?"

"I don't know." Tony hesitated. "She doesn't jitter, and she's got some sense."

Rette was all ears, though she kept her eyes on her book. If only she could find out what boys like Tony admired in girls, maybe she—

"How about my bringing her here for supper some night?" Tony was saying, as he stretched his long legs and fastened his eyes on his shoes.

"Any time," said Mrs. Larkin calmly, as though it weren't unusual for Tony to suggest bringing a girl home. But Rette looked up in surprise and caught a flicker of interest in her mother's eye.

"Maybe next week end," said Tony. "Friday or Saturday."

"Just let me know."

Rette closed her book and said: "Guess I'll go to bed. I'll be home late tomorrow, Mother. I'm going out to the airport, you know."

Tony looked up quizzically. "Airport?"

"Rette's class is making a field trip to the new airport," her mother said.

Tony didn't pursue the subject, so Rette went upstairs and laid out clean underwear, the newest of her school sweaters, and a Scotch plaid skirt that had been a Christmas present. With a mild and pleasant sense of participation, she was ready to greet the new day.

Fortunately, Monday's temperature bettered Sunday's by ten degrees. The sun shone with pale promise of spring and the bus—a big one—was crowded. Margaret had not come, but Elise was there, and Judy, along with a crowd of junior and senior girls who had frankly come just for the ride and the opportunity of seeing that glamorous Mr. Irish again. Jeff Chandler was sitting with Larry Carpenter, and, as Rette had predicted, Corky Adams and one of his cronies shared the seat just ahead.

Loretta couldn't help wondering who, in this group, would actually try for the prize. She hadn't realized that so many Avondale High students were even superficially interested in flying, and she considered the situation soberly as the bus rolled up School Street and down the highway, past the entrance to Cherry Tree Road and into the country beyond.

Barely half a mile from the edge of town, the driver turned into a winding secondary road that led past the Tisdale farm. No longer, however, were the flat fields covered with barley and winter wheat. As the driver slowed down to turn along the eastern boundary of the former farm, Rette could see a wind tee directly in front of her and an air strip which ran down almost to the road itself.

In the distance, near the farmhouse, which had been left standing, was a newly completed hangar and a couple of low buildings still under construction. Everything, to the high-school crowd, looked very raw and new.

Judy said, "Doesn't look like much, does it?" and Rette was about to agree reluctantly when she caught sight of a plane taxiing down the strip toward the starting point, only a few yards from the road they were now traveling.

"Hey! That's a new Stinson Voyager!" Rette heard Corky shout, as the plane reached the end of the strip.

The plane turned, headed into the wind, and the pilot started his take-off run. No sooner was he off the ground and climbing for altitude than a Piper Cruiser glided in, about twenty-five feet above the bus, and gently settled down onto the runway.

At the roar of the motor, so close above his head, the bus driver pretended to duck. "Boy, this is a busy spot!" he said as he turned the long bus into the airport drive. "Wouldn't think people'd be anxious to go up in the air, cold as it is."

Rette felt a shiver of sympathy crawl down her spine— or was it a shiver of excitement? She climbed down from the bus alongside the hangar and followed the faculty member in charge of the expedition across a cleared area to the old farmhouse, outside of which hung a new sign, with the word "OFFICE" lettered in black.

Stephen Irish met them at the door, looking more rugged than ever in flying clothes. He pushed forth his lower lip and grinned when he saw the size of the crowd. "Glad to see you," he called, with a gesture akin to a salute. "We might as well begin our conducted tour right here."

54

Along with the rest, Rette crowded into the office, where Mr. Irish divided the group into two, turning one section over to a flying instructor he introduced as Andy Keller. Andy was a rawboned young man, as homely as Mr. Irish was handsome, but Rette rather liked his appealing, mongrel-pup look, and wasn't too disappointed to find herself in his group.

The next half hour was interesting. Andy explained to his followers the traffic pattern of the airport, a diagram of which was hanging on one wall of the office. He told them that with a northerly wind, the pilot used the north-south runway, and pointed out the importance of the wind tee in deciding the take-off direction.

Rette listened carefully, but found much that the young man said as meaningless as one of the problems in algebra with which she so frequently struggled. The hangar and the actual planes harbored there interested her far more. She had a dozen questions on the tip of her tongue, but none of the girls seemed to be doing any talking, so she restrained herself.

Andy showed them a Piper Cub, describing its action and its parts as he led the group around it. Rette's head was buzzing with words that were new to her—aileron, fin, jury struts, elevator. Flying sounded much more complicated, even, than she had imagined. Who was it that had been telling her dad it wasn't much harder than driving a car?

At the end of the separate tours, Mr. Irish took over and talked to the entire group briefly. "One of you," he said, touching with a caressing gesture the wing of a trim little Cessna by which he stood, "is going to have a chance to fly one of these planes. The first time you feel that stick move in your hand will be one of the thrills of your lifetime. And when you come to solo—" Words were inadequate. He let the unfinished sentence hang in the air.

"I'm wishing you luck, each one of you who decides to enter the contest. If you've got a real yen to fly, and an average gift of gab, go to it. And here's a tip. Keep what you write about flying *well within your own world*. Keep it sincere." He tipped an imaginary hat. "And I'll be seein' you!"

CHAPTER SEVEN

"Well within your own world."

Rette pondered the flyer's words on Saturday morning as she sat at the low pine desk in her bedroom, her legs wrapped around a Hitchcock chair that had come from Gramp's house on King Street.

In front of her was a sheaf of yellow copy paper such as the staff of the *Arrow* used, and between her even teeth was the end of a pencil, thoroughly chewed.

She wished she knew what Mr. Irish had really meant by that remark. Like the title chosen for the essay contest, it seemed ambiguous. Rette looked at the single sentence on the paper before her and sighed.

"From stories and legends handed down through the years, we know that even from earliest times people have dreamed of flying."

She knew. All week Rette had been haunting the reference room of the public library. She knew about Daedalus and Icarus and Hermes and the legends surrounding their attempts to fly. She knew that Archimedes and later Roger Bacon and Leonardo da Vinci had believed in airships. She knew that in 1678 Besnier, a French locksmith, had constructed a curious flying machine with wooden shoulder bars and muslin wings.

She had read everything she could find on the beginnings of aviation, on the early dreamers preceding the Montgolfier brothers, who made the first successful attempt to fly in 1783 with their hot-air balloon. She was full of her subject, yet everything she wrote seemed static to her. She wanted to get the lift, the thrill, of the idea of flight into her writing. But the words stood still.

Rette frowned, wadded the sheet of paper into a ball, and tossed it to settle in the wastebasket on top of a congregation of its fellows. Then she sighed again, quite audibly.

The sound was like a signal to Gramp. Rette could hear his chair scrape back and a second later his feet began their halting shuffle across the hall.

"Working?" His voice was full of invitation and his eyes were hopeful as he popped his head in at Rette's door.

"Sort of." Rette leaned back in her chair. "I'm trying to start this essay on flying, Gramp."

"Flying?" Gramp's memory was short these days.

Rette explained, while Gramp leaned against the doorjamb. "You really want to learn to fly, Lark?" he asked.

Loretta nodded. "More than ever, now that I've been out to the airport."

"Like Tony."

"I guess so," Rette admitted. "Do you think it's funny, for a girl?"

"No," said Gramp at once. "No, of course not. Girls drive cars, don't they? What's funny about that?"

Loretta grinned. "Gramp, you're wonderful!" It was comforting to know that in the eyes of at least one person, she could do no wrong.

The old man came in and sat down on the edge of Rette's high-post bed. His granddaughter swung around, straddling her chair.

"Now what is it you have to write about?" Gramp asked.

"'The Dream of Flying,'" Rette repeated.

"And how many times have you been to the airport?" Gramp asked.

"Once."

"Not enough," he said immediately. "You ought to go out and hang around awhile. You can't get ideas sitting here cooped up in your room."

"But—but wouldn't I feel silly?" Gramp was a person to whom Rette could speak her thoughts.

"What if you do? Though I don't see why you should. Talk to the fellas out there, the mechanics and all of 'em. That's what I used to do, when I was a boy—hang around the automobiles." His eyes looked back over the years and he made a confession. "I was crazy as a young loon about cars."

But Rette was already looking out of the window. The weather had become gradually warmer all week, until now, on Saturday, there was a softness in the air that betokened a false spring before the winds of March blew winter back again.

"Got to soak up a subject," Gramp was saying. "Got to be full of it." He was sounding the death knell to his hopes for a pinochle game, but he was doing it for his favorite grandchild.

Rette took his advice. She made herself a couple of sandwiches and ate them standing at the kitchen table before she got out her bike and pedaled to the airport. If she saw Mr. Irish, she promised herself, she'd ask him what he meant by his advice to the contestants. But it wasn't Mr. Irish she ran into as she rode along the edge of the landing field. It was Jeff Chandler, who was leaning against the wheel of his own bicycle, watching with great interest a plane that was just turning to take off.

Rette would have ridden right on past him, but Jeff turned at the crunch of wheels on the gravel road and said, "Hi," as though he were surprised to see her there.

"Hi," Rette replied, then made the sort of inane remark which she despised in others. "Feel's like spring, doesn't it?"

Jeff mumbled something affirmative and said, "If you had your choice, what kind of plane would you like to fly?"

"Why, I don't know. I hadn't thought," Rette replied quite truthfully. One small plane looked much like another to her.

But Jeff, at such an admission, looked grieved. He turned back to watching the plane, which was now in the air, and Rette, interpreting this action as dismissal, rode on.

Around the airport buildings, Rette found a good deal of activity. Several light planes had been wheeled out of the hangars, and mechanics in coveralls were working on them. A couple of men were sitting on the office steps, smoking and talking. A Bellanca was being gassed up almost directly in front of them, and as Rette leaned her bike against the porch she could hear one of them comment on it.

"That's Charlie Kenton's plane, isn't it?"

The other man considered. "Yep, think it is. The Kentons are flying up to Newburgh for a wedding this afternoon." He glanced at his watch. "Ought to be leaving about now."

He glanced back toward the office door, which was just opening, then nodded affirmatively to his friend. Rette watched while a young woman in a tweed suit, with a fur coat over her arm and a traveling bag in one hand, came out on the porch and squinted into the sun at the plane.

The men on the steps stood up, and the woman nodded and smiled. "Beautiful flying weather," she said happily. A minute later she was joined by her husband and Stephen Irish, with whom she seemed to be on friendly terms.

Rette could hear her say as they walked to the plane: "Charlie's got his top hat and his skis. We're going on up to Vermont for a couple of days if the weather holds."

They were starting off with no more ado than if they had been going by car. Rette felt as though she were standing agape, from the sheer wonder of it. It was interesting, she reflected, that she had seen the same sort of thing in the movies dozens of times and had not been in the least impressed. But this Mrs. Kenton looked so normal and unaffected. And she was real flesh and blood, a person Rette could have reached out and touched. It made a difference, enough difference to set a thrill of excitement chasing down her spine.

She watched the plane taxiing in shallow S-turns to the take-off point, heard the distant swelling of the motor, and followed the ship with her eyes as it rose with the easy grace of a gull, climbing and turning, the wings catching the bright winter sunlight. She shaded her eyes with her hand and followed its flight until it was a pin point in the distance. When she brought her gaze back to earth, Mr. Irish was standing a few yards from her.

He nodded, and jerked his head toward the disappearing plane. "Romantic, isn't it?"

Rette agreed, marveling at his apparent ability to read her mind.

He looked at her more closely. "Weren't you here with the high-school group?"

"Yes," Rette told him, "I was."

"What's your name?"

"Loretta Larkin."

"Oh, yes. Your dad's in the real-estate business in town." Rette nodded.

"And you have a brother who flew in the war. Let's see—"

"Tony," Rette told him. "He was with the 82d Airborne." She couldn't keep the pride out of her voice.

Mr. Irish snapped his fingers. "Sure! I was certain that name rang a bell. Is he still flying?"

"Just with the Reserve. He's got a job with an oil company, selling." It seemed to Rette that she was always telling somebody or other this dismal fact.

"You sound dismayed." Mr. Irish was grinning now.

"I guess I am, a little. It's like you said—flying's a romantic sort of business. Oil's—well—dull."

Now the man laughed out loud. "Some of the boys in the West would be pretty surprised to hear you say that," he told Rette. Then he started up the office steps. "I'd better get back to work or I'll be fired," he said over his shoulder. Then, at the door, he looked back again. "You out here picking up atmosphere?" he asked with amusement.

Rette flushed. "Well, sort of." She didn't meet his eyes.

"Help yourself," Stephen Irish told her. "Ramble around. Ask questions if you can find anybody to answer 'em. Just saw another one of your gang back by the supply room. Nice-looking boy. Tall. I don't know his name."

"That's Jeff Chandler," Rette told him, but he was already closing the door.

Rette wandered around, but she didn't ask questions. She just looked. When she saw Jeff in the distance, she deliberately avoided him, because she was sure that if they got into conversation again she'd say something else to give her away as an ignoramus. Jeff probably knew the names of planes the way some boys know the name of every car on the road.

It was obvious that Jeff didn't share Rette's reluctance to talk to the mechanics. She saw him in conversation with several of the men, and more often than not he seemed to have his head poked into the cockpit or under the fuselage of a plane. She had a feeling that he was asking intelligent questions, and it rather worried her. After a while she decided to go home.

It was so warm by now that she took off her mittens and tossed them into her bicycle basket. She even unbuttoned her reversible coat and let it hang loose, with the plaid lining a bright streak of color against her dark-green sweater and skirt. She pedaled along the road that led back to Avondale in a leisurely fashion, humming to herself and rather glad to be alone in the welcome sunshine. She was just turning into King Street when Jeff passed her, riding fast. He waved to her over his shoulder, seemed to brake as though he were about to pull in and wait for her, then apparently thought better of it and rode on.

At the next corner, where Cherry Tree Road cut in at an angle, Rette caught up to Jeff again. He was walking now, balancing his bicycle with one hand as he talked to Elise and Judy, who were apparently headed downtown. Both girls were laughing, and Elise was nodding knowingly.

"Apple-polishing! Isn't that what they called it in the Army? A fine thing!" Rette heard her say.

"Nothing of the sort!" Jeff retorted, not in the least daunted by Elise's teasing. Then he caught sight of Rette out of the corner of his eye. "You can ask Rette Larkin! She's the one who was making time with Irish. All he did when he saw me was grunt."

Rette pulled up, ready to contradict him with the best grace she could muster, but blushing in spite of herself.

"Loretta!" Judy squealed before she could open her mouth. "You sly thing! Pretending you don't like boys and then cottoning up to Mr. Irish!" She shook a remonstrative finger and struck a pose.

Jeff, quite ready to pass the buck, winked with great meaning and said, "That's right!"

The girls were being absurd, and Rette knew it. They

didn't mean to be unkind, particularly, but on the other hand it didn't concern them to sense that she was embarrassed. There was only one way to handle the situation cleverly. It was her cue to make a flip retort and laugh it off.

"But naturally!" Elise would have said in her place. "Older men are just my dish!" She would have ridden away with a fillip and the echo of amused laughter in her ears.

But Rette wasn't Elise. With every passing second she felt less and less able to cope with such raillery. Everybody in Avondale High knew that the boys automatically passed Rette Larkin by. Even joking about a hypothetical crush on the glamorous Mr. Irish was, Rette felt, making her look ridiculous. While she sat on the saddle of her bike, rowing along with one foot on the curb and a grin frozen on her face, she could feel hot resentment rising in her throat until it threatened to choke her. Any chance to save the day was lost.

"I don't really blame her," Elise was saying to Jeff and Judy in the same light, teasing tone. "Stephen Irish is just about *the* most attractive character in these-here parts. Give, Rette. What's your technique? Do you go all soft and starry-eyed or do you treat him like a brother?"

Rette was really on the defensive now. Fury was replacing resentment, and she knew that her eyes had hardened and her jaw had set.

"Don't be simple-minded," she snapped, her husky voice sounding rough and boyish. "Mr. Irish doesn't even know my first name."

"He does too!" Jeff crowed, goaded on because she had risen so beautifully to the bait. "I heard you tell him. I was walking right behind you, so I know!"

Rette shot him a look of pure venom, while the girls burst into laughter.

"Rette!" Judy chided, and waggled her finger again.

But Rette was riding away.

"O Rette, don't be mad! We were just teasing," Elise called after her, but she didn't look back. She stood on her pedals and raced up Cherry Tree Road without dignity, hating herself for turning tail but hating Jeff and Elise and Judy even more.

They were childish. They were stupid. They were deliberately turning a knife in the very spot they knew to be vulnerable. She gave them no benefit of the doubt, as a less intense person might have. Her cheeks beet red with shame and anger, she slammed her bike against the side of the garage and fled through the back door and up the kitchen stairs to the solace of her own room.

Gramp, who had been dozing, heard her. He came to the closed door but refrained from opening it.

"Lark," he called, "you home?"

Rette's reply was affirmative but muffled.

"Did you have fun?"

"Oh, swell fun!"

Rette did her best to sound normal, and hoped that Gramp couldn't detect the edge of bitterness in her voice.

CHAPTER EIGHT

For a week of nights Loretta worked as she had never worked before. She let her homework slide while she concentrated on the essay. She wrote and rewrote. In disgust she tore up what she had written and tried again.

She outlined elaborately, trying to give her writing some structure. Then she worked with stern concentration on her phrasing, searching for just the right word to interpret a thought, spending precious half hours with the dictionary, doing her utmost to create a better than average job, a composition that would impress the judges, an essay that would *win!*

Finally, she typed the completed manuscript laboriously on her father's old portable Corona, making it look neat and professional, to Gramp's delight.

"At-a-girl, Lark!" he commended her. "Do it up brown."

Meanwhile, life at school and home slid past Loretta as water past a stone in a slow-flowing brook. She put the incident that had followed the excursion to the airport out of her mind, but she went to some pains to avoid Elise and Judy. Jeff she didn't especially condemn.

The closing date for the essay contest was March 15, and Rette still had ten days' leeway when she typed, "Loretta Larkin, 120 Cherry Tree Road, Avondale," at the top of her cover sheet. She wasn't displeased with the manuscript. It was knowledgeable, almost erudite, for a girl of sixteen. Only one thing bothered her. It didn't seem to have much life.

She showed it to her mother, and Mrs. Larkin read it carefully. "You've certainly done a lot of research," she said.

She showed it to Gramp, who was keenly interested, but she didn't get a very encouraging response. "I don't know, Lark," he said apologetically. "I'm an old fellow. It sounds very dressed-up and impressive, but there's a lot that doesn't really mean much to me."

Rette wanted to show it to Tony, but she was strangely bashful. Anything she could possibly write about flying seemed so trivial. She was afraid he'd laugh at her, or, worse yet, patronize her, although he never had.

One thing continued to bother her. The phrase *"within your own world"* was like a haunting refrain in her mind. She didn't think her carefully polished efforts quite met those specifications, but then she didn't understand quite what the caution meant.

On Sunday night, a week from the day Rette had started serious work on the essay, Ellen Alden came to supper as Tony's guest.

It was a night of storm, with snow spatting against the windows and the consequent sense of warmth and coziness within. Tony had built the fire in the living room himself, hauling in extra wood to bank in the basket that stood beside the brick hearth. The table was laid with green linen, and there were white candles in the Victorian, grape-wreathed candelabra. Gramp had put on his newest smoking jacket, a Christmas present from the family.

"Got to do Tony proud," he said, brushing at his lapels. "Means something, to be bringing home a girl."

Rette's eyebrows lowered a little. "What does it mean?" She sounded so contentious that Gramp felt abashed.

"In my day," he said, "it meant you were introducing her to the family. But maybe times have changed."

Rette didn't want to like Ellen Alden. She would have denied any feeling of jealousy, yet buried within her was a desire to keep Tony for the family, for herself, not to share him with some strange girl.

Yet when Ellen came through the front door, smiling and clapping the snow from her white fur mittens, tugging at the cord that fastened her hooded coat, she was so alive and so winning that Rette could feel her truculence die.

"Here," she offered, holding out her hands for the coat, "let me take that."

Ellen captivated the entire family, Gramp included. There was a naturalness about her, as Tony had said, that put everyone at ease. It wasn't until after supper that Rette happened to get into conversation with her alone. Then the two girls found themselves clearing the table together while Mrs. Larkin stacked dishes in the kitchen and Tony went out for more firewood.

"Tell me," Ellen said, "did Tony like the book?"

"I think so," Rette replied. "He's been reading it, off and on. But I don't think he has finished it yet."

Ellen nodded. "It's a book to read slowly," she said.

"I've read parts of it," Rette said. "It's different."

Ellen turned back to the table from putting the silver salt dishes on the buffet. "It is," she agreed. Then she smiled again. "I remember the day you came into the bookstore—and the wind blew the door out of your hand."

"Don't remind me!"

"You wanted so much to find just the *right* book. You were so earnest and so pretty, with your big dark eyes and that bright bandanna—" Ellen paused, "Why, what's the matter?"

Rette couldn't explain that her mouth had dropped

68

open from sheer astonishment. Nobody, except Gramp, had called her "pretty" for as long as she could recall.

"Nothing," she covered clumsily, picking up the candle snuffer. "I was just amazed that you'd remember me at all."

A few minutes later Ellen proposed, "Let's us do the dishes, Rette," and persuaded Mrs. Larkin out of the kitchen, so that Rette and she were alone again.

Now, searching for a topic of conversation, Rette told her about the contest, with flying lessons as the prize. Ellen was easy to talk to, because she was so interested in everything. She wanted to know the essay subject, and repeated it thoughtfully.

"Not too easy, to write about intangibles," she said.

Grateful that Ellen was talking to her as though they were on the same level, Rette expanded still farther and mentioned the phrase that had been haunting her thoughts.

"Keep it 'well within your own world,' Mr. Irish said. What do you suppose he meant by that?"

"I think I know," Ellen said promptly, leaning against a table with a dish she was drying forgotten in her hand, "but it's not an easy thing to explain." She thought a minute. "Have you ever had an English teacher tell you to write about things you know?"

Rette nodded. "Of course. But I don't *know* anything about flying. None of us do, really. We just want to learn."

"You're writing about the *dream* of flying. You know something about that." Ellen put down the dish, took up another, and looked at Rette thoughtfully. "I'd like to give you a book, if you'll stop in at the shop after school tomorrow. It's a book you should read anyway, and this may be just the time. It was written by a college girl who would have understood exactly what Mr. Irish meant."

Rette expected a book on flying, but when she took the

red-jacketed book that Ellen held out to her the next afternoon she read the title in surprise. "*Seventeenth Summer*," it said.

"Why—this is a novel!"

Ellen nodded. "A good one. You'll love it."

Curiously, Rette riffled the pages, then turned to the blurb on the back. The picture of a girl, vividly Irish, with a wealth of dark hair and with eyes that were probably the color of periwinkle, looked up at her.

"Maureen Daly," Rette read. "Is *she* the author? She looks so young!"

Ellen laughed. "She was only nineteen when she wrote this story. I'm anxious to hear what you think of it. Most people agree that she's managed to do a pretty remarkable thing."

Ellen had the ability to fire others with her own enthusiasm, and while Loretta still couldn't conceive what possible connection this novel about a girl's first love might have with her own essay on flying, she hurried through her homework that night and went to bed early, taking the book with her.

"A deplorable habit, reading in bed," her dad always said. "Bad for your eyes, bad for your posture, bad for everything." Yet both Rette and her mother persisted in the unhealthy habit and even cherished it. "My only vice," Mrs. Larkin told her husband firmly. "I think you should be indulgent."

There is nothing, Rette thought, as she adjusted the shade on her bedside lamp and snuggled down under the covers, quite like starting a brand-new book. The book has to be fresh, preferably unread, so that the smell of printer's ink and new paper still clings to it. The binding should be unbroken, and the jacket shouldn't be dog-eared or torn. Even the first sentence is full of promise. No other feeling is quite like this.

And no other book that she had ever read, Rette decided after an hour, had quite the quality of *Seventeenth Summer*. There was a homeliness, a deep-rooted honesty, a youthfulness about it that made Loretta catch her breath. She didn't live in the sort of town Angie Morrow lived in; she didn't have that sort of family; she had yet to have a love affair. Yet the story was so real and so fresh that Rette *became* Angie. She shared every feeling, every impulse, every hope and every thrill and every disappointment.

How can this be, she wondered? And then she decided that it was because the author was so close to her subject that she knew infallibly how to take her heroine every step of the way. She was writing about something out of her own intimate experience—within her own world.

Rette let the book lie on the coverlet and clasped her hands behind her head. She knew now why Gramp had called her writing "dressed-up." He meant that it was pompous. For the first time she began to think of writing not as an exercise in word arrangement, but as an effort to capture life and truth in simple terms on paper.

It doesn't matter what a person writes about, Rette decided, as long as it's something she knows. It doesn't matter how conventional or unconventional a person's terms are, so long as the language fits the subjects, so long as it rings true!

She heard the car roll up the drive, and into the garage, heard the slamming of the doors, the entry of her mother and father into the house. A few minutes later there were quick, light feet on the stairs and Mrs. Larkin pushed Rette's door open a crack.

"Are you still reading?" There was the gentlest sort of reprimand in her tone.

"Just stopped." Rette countered with another question. "Was the movie good?"

"So-so." Her mother dropped down for a moment on the

71

edge of Rette's bed, unbuttoning the throat of her fly-front wool sport dress. "Some of the situations Hollywood dreams up are so artificial, or maybe Dad and I are just getting old."

Rette laughed. Her mother looked far from old.

"If you want an antidote, you ought to read the book I'm reading. It's awfully good."

Mrs. Larkin picked up the book and glanced at the title. "*Seventeenth Summer.* Where did you get this?"

"Ellen gave it to me. I don't know quite why she should be so generous, but it's a wonderful book!"

Mrs. Larkin's eyebrows raised impishly, and she smiled. "Ellen," she said, "is a clever girl."

"Why?"

"Winning over Tony's young sister is part of the game." Rette was shocked. "O Mother, she wouldn't!"

"Why wouldn't she?" asked Mrs. Larkin. "I did." She leaned back and hugged one knee with her hands. "I remember the first time I met Dad's family. I wanted them to like me—desperately! And I think they did, except for Peter. It took me months and a trip to the shore to win him over. But it was worth it."

"Uncle Pete didn't like you?" Rette was incredulous. Her dad's younger brother adored his sister-in-law now.

"He thought I was an interloper. He was as crazy about George as—as you are about Tony. He thought no girl could possibly be good enough for his brother." Mrs. Larkin smiled again.

"But—but, Mother. You don't think, with Tony, there's anything really serious?" She paused, trying to accustom herself to such an idea.

"I hope there is," replied her mother confidentially. "Ellen is a fine girl, attractive, levelheaded, and feminine enough to be artful. Tony could go far and do a great deal worse."

"You mean—you'd like him to *marry* her?"

Mrs. Larkin's eyes twinkled and she pursed her lips in a little *moue*. "I would."

While Loretta regarded her in frank astonishment, Mrs. Larkin leaned on one elbow and tried to explain. "Tony needs to be married, Rette. You're old enough to understand. He's mature for his years. The war has seen to that. He's high-strung and affectionate and he's—" she waved her free hand, seeking for a word—"he's sort of foot-loose right now. He's outgrown us, Rette. He's a man, and he should have his own home and his own life."

After her mother had left, Rette lay in the darkness and thought about their conversation for a long time. She was proud to be taken into her mother's confidence; it made her feel adult and responsible. But she still couldn't quite face the probability of Tony's marriage. When she contemplated the gap it would leave in the household, it made her stomach feel empty and aching. She didn't want him to go away—with Ellen or any other girl.

Rette recognized the sensation of emptiness. She had experienced it first when she was six, and her mother had gone off for a week on a trip with a friend. Dad was home, and so was Tony, along with a temporary housekeeper, but it wasn't the same without Mother. Rette had wandered around the place like a lost puppy, feeling miserable and alone.

Again, but to a lesser degree, Rette had felt desolate when Tony went off to war. Pride had bolstered her courage then, along with the firm belief that he would soon be home again.

Marriage, however, was final, too final to contemplate. Restlessly, Rette punched at her pillow. Life was getting too complicated entirely. Between Tony and the essay contest and her own inner confusion she felt tossed and pommeled.

73

And that wasn't all! There was a basketball game tomorrow, and her algebra grades were still in the depths, and spring sports were already being talked about at school. Rette wondered whether things semed so critical to older people. She decided they didn't. Older people seemed to develop a sort of crust, through which their feelings never quite bubbled. In a way that would be comfortable, but in another way it would be upsetting. She was afraid that when the bubbling stopped, so would the sense of feeling vitally alive.

CHAPTER NINE

During the next two days it rained with dreary persistence. Then a March wind whipped the rain to ice on the sidewalks of Avondale and everybody kept saying, "Isn't this miserable weather?" But Rette didn't notice.

Rette was in Fond du Lac with Angie Morrow, enwrapped in a summer romance that was mysterious and sweet and exciting, and so real that the experience didn't seem vicarious at all.

Seventeenth Summer went everywhere with Loretta until she finished it. The book was opened behind her *American History* in study hall; it found its way into English class and replaced *Algebra III* on her desk at night. On Wednesday evening, when Rette came to the end, she heaved a languishing sigh. She wanted the story to go right on, like the series books of her childhood.

The amazing part of it was that Angie Morrow and Jack Duluth didn't seem like book characters at all. They were just like any girl and boy that Rette might be going to school with, except that she knew more about them, about the way they thought and felt, than she did about any of her friends.

At first all Rette's consciousness was so much part of the story that she couldn't analyze the writing, couldn't consider it dispassionately, as Ellen had intended that she should. But gradually she began to see that the author had captured, with extraordinary sensitivity, an experience that, because of its very nature, no older writer could have touched. She had written about something only possible within her own youthful world.

On Thursday, before dinner, Rette read over her essay for the contest and, compared with Maureen Daly's writing, it seemed stupid and stale. She consoled herself that no essay could possibly duplicate the natural style of such a novel; but, later, as she sat at the table and listened to her family's routine conversation, she was preoccupied. What had Ellen expected of her, she wondered? Why, at what seemed to Rette to be the eleventh hour, had she insisted that she read this book?

Gramp was trying to break into her reverie. "Lark," Rette awoke to hear him saying, "isn't tomorrow the big day?"

"What big day?" As though Rette didn't know perfectly well that the fifteenth was the due date for the essay.

"'Beware the ides of March'!" Gramp quoted in a stentorian voice, not put off by her question, and because the rest of the family began to look at her, Rette pushed back her chair and grumbled: "Oh, you mean the essay! I think I'm going to skip it. I haven't got a chance anyway."

But after dinner, instead of doing her homework, she shut herself in her bedroom and put a clean sheet of copy paper into her dad's typewriter.

"The Dream of Flying," she wrote at the top.

Then, for a long while, she just sat.

How would it sound, she wondered, if she really wrote about flying from her heart, if she tried to put down, in all honesty, the dream that was hers and that must have been, to a fullness that her mind could not encompass, the dream of every man who ever dared think of conquering the air?

She let her thoughts drift, and she was filled with a strange elation, a sense of power that was new to her, that had nothing to do with the feeling she had on the basketball court or when she held a tennis racket in her hand.

Finally, halting every few words, she started to put sentences on the blank paper.

"Everything important that has ever happened," she began simply, "first of all was a dream.

"Every great painting was once a dream in the artist's eye. Every book is a dream, every building. If we couldn't dream, we wouldn't keep on growing. Our world would just stop."

Rette paused and sat with her hands in her lap staring into space.

"The dream of flying," she wrote after a while, "is thousands of years old, and yet it is as young as a little boy watching the flight of his first homemade glider. Daedalus and Leonardo and Besnier were the visionaries. Octave Chanute and the Wright brothers took up their dreams and made them into fact."

She paused again, thinking of her own dream of flying, which had begun in the days when she had sat beside Tony's worktable, watching him fashion model airplanes with infinite care. She remembered a time when he was a smooth-faced lad in corduroy pants and she was in first grade, just learning to read. He had waved an unfinished model in her face one day and said, very firmly, "Someday I'm going to fly one of these jobs."

"Me too," she had promised, just as firmly, because everything that Tony did she had wanted to do.

The door opened gently, and Gramp's head appeared and retreated, but Rette didn't hear or see. Dreams have curious beginnings, she thought, and tried to put something of her own dream of learning to fly down on paper, not trying to sound original, but writing about her early desire to emulate Tony in a frank and unvarnished way.

Then, because it seemed to follow naturally, she wrote about the war, and the years in which her beautiful dream of flying had turned into a nightmare of wordless fear for her brother. But Tony had come home, with his own faith in the air still high, and Rette had begun to dream again.

She wrote about the way her trips to the airport made her heart quicken, the lift and urgency she felt as she watched an ascending plane, the keen thrill of her first flight, when she had looked down on a tidy, spacious earth from the strange and delightful viewpoint of a bird.

But that trip in a commercial air liner she recognized as nothing in comparison to the thrill of learning to master a small plane. Then, suddenly, her experience stopped. Her story ended, but not her dream.

"For I shall always dream of flying," she finished, "as long as I am young."

When she took the last sheet of paper out of the typewriter Rette felt suddenly tired. Her back ached and her eyes were heavy. She couldn't even bear to think of reading over what she had written, she was so anxious to get in bed.

The next morning she overslept, and gathered up the papers on her desk hastily, slipping both the new and old versions of her essay between the pages of her blackbound notebook. She'd read them over, she decided, and make a decision between them, when she got to school.

The rain had stopped, but the bare limbs of the trees were still coated with melting ice, and drops of water hit the pavement with a monotonous rhythm. There was a dull red blush of buds along the maple branches, but

Rette didn't discover this precursor of spring. She felt listless and heavy and uncomfortably aware that she had done no homework at all, not even math. Gone entirely was the stimulation of last night.

When she reread the newer version of her essay, she felt even worse. It was simple, all right—so simple that it seemed childish. It also seemed disturbingly intimate. How could she have thought that all that stuff about Tony and herself had any meaning? She slapped the papers back between the leaves of the notebook and began sorting books for her morning classes with a dismal sense of inadequacy.

"Maureen Daly," she muttered, "my eye!"

"What did you say?" asked Corky, from behind her.

"Nothing," Rette returned.

"Well, you needn't be disagreeable."

"And you needn't be nosy," Rette shot back without a smile.

The drone of familiar voices laboring through French translation soothed her a little. They were reading *La Tulipe Noire,* and Rette found the story easy enough to follow, even without preparation. Her French vocabulary had always been good, and she never had much trouble in hitting upon apt English synonyms. But when she entered Mr. Scott's room her heart fell to the soles of her saddle shoes. He was writing questions on the blackboard for what was obviously a sprung quiz.

Rette hadn't cracked an algebra book for a week now. Between one thing and another—reading and writing, to be exact—there just hadn't been time. The problems posed looked more like Greek than anything she had previously encountered. They were tolling a death knell to a place on the tennis team. Rette's ears positively rang with the imagined sound.

Through half the period she sat making meaningless

79

marks on paper so that she would look busy. Then she simply sat, facing the fact that this situation couldn't go on. She'd have to confess to Mr. Scott that she had fallen hopelessly behind, and she'd have to face his inevitable suggestion—a tutor. How she could ever broach the subject of a tutor to her family, who had always exhibited the most trusting confidence in her brains, she didn't at the moment know.

At the end of the period Rette crumpled the test paper in her hand and dropped it into the wastebasket at the front of the classroom. She waited until the rest of the pupils had left, then approached Mr. Scott.

"I'm not handing in a paper," she told him. "Things seem to have gone from bad to worse. I guess I'll have to have some help if I'm ever going to pass this course."

Mr. Scott didn't have to tell Rette that in her senior year such a situation was serious. She knew. He looked at her quietly and said, "You mean you'd like me to suggest a tutor?" and mutely Rette nodded her head.

Mr. Scott consulted some names in the back of his roll book. "I'm all filled up," he told her, "and so is Miss Carpenter. There are some senior boys who have asked for some tutoring work though. I'll have to see who can take you on."

Rette felt as though her face had turned brick red. This was real humiliation—to be tutored by a classmate, and a boy at that!

"Couldn't one of the other teachers—" she started, but Mr. Scott was already shaking his head. "Spring is always a crowded time. I'll do the best I can for you, Loretta. If you really apply yourself, I think a couple of extra hours a week should see you through."

As Rette walked up the stairs to the auditorium, where she had a period of study hall, she could just imagine the sort of tutor she'd draw—somebody like Corky, bespec-

tacled and smug about his superior knowledge, who
would even rather enjoy lording it over a girl whom he
considered uppity anyway.

She tried to take her mind off her ill fortune by reading
both her essays over again. Definitely, now, she decided
that the first one was far superior to her last-minute effort
of the night before. She folded them both lengthwise and
tucked them into the back of her history book. When she
next walked past the principal's office, she'd drop the
chosen theme into the entry box. Not, in her present state
of discouragement, that she thought it had much of a
chance.

Lunch hour followed study hall, and Rette went directly to the cafeteria, where the girls were now strangely
silent on the subject of the contest. No one seemed willing
to admit that she was or was not entering a manuscript.
Apparently they felt that either stand would be incrimi-
nating. Rette played along with the crowd and kept silent
about her plans too.

The boys were less shy. Noisy banter came from the
tables in the corner where Jeff Chandler and his crowd
always sat. Apparently Jeff was the favorite, among the
entries, because big Bill Jenkins, who always tried to get
somebody to bet with him on every game and every con-
troversy involving Avondale High, was laying two to one
that Jeff would win and finding no takers.

Only Elise, among the girls, finally decided to be ex-
pansive. "I tried and tried," she admitted, "but I couldn't
seem to get a thing on paper that made good sense. I
guess I'm just not a writer. Anyway, the prize really ought
to go to a boy."

"That's right," agreed Dora Phillips, who always sup-
ported Elise in everything, "a girl would feel sort of silly
winning a prize like that, don't you think?"

"Why?" Rette wanted to ask, from her seat several

81

places down the long table, but she knew it would only make her sound belligerent. She bit her lower lip and kept her peace.

"Oh, I don't know," Elise was saying calmly. "I'd be thrilled."

Silently Rette cheered. Every once in a while Elise came up with something, in a quiet, offhand way, with which Rette agreed heartily. Then she forgot her jealousy and almost liked the girl. Almost.

After lunch Cathy and Rette walked over to the gym together, and Rette told Cathy about the algebra test and the prospect of a tutor. Cathy, as usual, was comforting.

"It does seem stupid, when you're so bright in everything else," she said. "But just because you *are* bright it ought to be a quick job to catch up."

Rette groaned. "You don't know me and math."

Cathy retorted with a laugh. "Stop being so *determined* that you can't do algebra," she said.

It was after her last class that Rette found herself in the corridor off which the principal's office opened. Well, it's now or never, she decided, and had her hand on the doorknob when a boy came up behind her, his rubber-soled shoes making no noise on the asphalt tile floor.

"About to cast the die?" Jeff Chandler asked.

Rette nodded. "You too?"

"Nope." Jeff shook his head. "My two cents' worth went in early this morning, before I lost my nerve. I'm just tracking you down, at the moment. Or haven't you heard?"

"Heard what?" Rette looked puzzled. She turned, her back to the door now, but one hand still clutching the knob. Her heart was beating faster than usual because any girl in Avondale High would be flattered to have Jeff Chandler searching her out. Just to have him standing in the corridor talking to her was exciting—she had to admit it. No matter why he had been looking for her, the fact that she could be seen with him gave her a certain feeling of prestige.

But his next words dashed any absurd hope she might have been harboring. "I'm supposed to tutor you in algebra," he said.

Rette was so shocked that she was temporarily speechless. Not Jeff Chandler! Oh, please, Mr. Scott—anybody but Jeff Chandler! Rette offered up a silent and ineffectual prayer.

If he weren't one of the most popular boys in the senior class, it would be different. Now Rette would gladly have settled for Corky or anybody else. But to have Jeff Chandler in the position of her mentor, to have to admit to him her abysmal ignorance of even the simplest algebraic problems, to be forced to accept doltishly his instruction —this, Rette felt sure, was the very depth of degradation. She wished she could quietly slip through the floor and disappear forever. The telltale red began to climb up her throat, in which a nervous pulse was beating. Her knuckles, behind her back, were white on the doorknob. Somehow, with pride that was almost a reflex, she kept her chin up.

"You'll be sorry," she said. "I'm awfully dumb."

The rest of the conversation Loretta could never quite remember. She realized that Jeff had suggested Tuesday and Thursday evenings and had arranged to come to her house at seven thirty each night. But the actual words that had passed between them were lost, because all she could think of at the time was her anxiety to get away.

Finally he walked off down the hall, with a casual, "I'll be seein' you," and Rette turned blindly into the office and tugged at one of the essays in the back of her history book, pushing it viciously into the slotted box.

It wasn't until Sunday night, when she opened her

American History to do her homework, that she realized the mistake she had made. The essay she had submitted to the contest was not the one she had decided upon. It was the second, last-minute attempt on which her chance for the prize would stand.

CHAPTER TEN

"No, I'm not going to the Senior Ball," Rette told her mother flatly a week later. "School dances are simply too dumb."

Mrs. Larkin looked confused and rather grieved. "But, Rette—" she began, then spread her hands in a small gesture of futility. "I mean, after all—your last year—"

Rette shrugged and ran upstairs whistling. Her only recourse was to pretend to ignore her mother's obvious concern. She couldn't admit that she wasn't going because nobody had asked her. She could only cloak her real feelings with assumed indifference, but she did wish people would let her alone!

It was like a conspiracy. Even Gramp was unconsciously involved in it. He came to his bedroom door waggling an admonitory finger.

"'Whistling girls and crowing hens,'" he quoted. There was no need to go on.

Rette went over and hugged him. "Now don't *you* start scolding me," she told him, "or I won't let you beat me at pinochle any more."

Gramp held her off and looked at her. "Me, scold you?" he asked innocently. "I've never scolded you in your life."

It was true. His occasional teasing was entirely without malice, and the fact that it occasionally struck home was sheer accident. Rette smiled and patted his cheek.

"You're an old smoothie," she said.

"What's a 'smoothie'?" Gramp asked.

"Apparently," Rette retorted cynically, "what I'm not."

Then, when he looked utterly confounded, she laughed at him and suggested generously, "Want to play a game with me right now?"

It relaxed Rette to be with Gramp. He demanded nothing of her but the pleasure of her company, and she felt warmed and softened by his love. But before the rest of the family she had to adopt an attitude of defiant unconcern. They kept bringing up subjects like the Senior Ball and Jeff Chandler, subjects that were loaded with dynamite, from Rette's point of view.

That evening Loretta was blocking a newly washed sweater on two turkish towels laid on her bed when her mother touched a match to the fuse. She wandered in with apparent casualness and said, "You know, Rette, that nice boy who has been tutoring you—I was thinking maybe he'd like to come a little early and have supper with us some night."

"And then again, maybe he wouldn't!" Rette straightened and whirled on her mother like an animal at bay. "Don't you dare ask him, ever! You promise."

"Why, Rette!"

"Look, Mother, Jeff's a big shot in the class. Besides, he's practically going steady with Elise." Rette wasn't sure whether this wasn't exaggeration, but at least it should end further discussion.

It did. Her mother said, "Oh!" in a vague sort of way and let the subject drop.

Her family's reaction to the announcement that she would have to be tutored in math had been far milder than Rette had anticipated. Her mother and dad had looked surprised and rather dismayed, but they hadn't upbraided her. Their attitude had been, "Let's get this thing straightened out as quickly as possible," and with forthright practicality they had discussed tutoring fees and the question of whether the two hours a week Mr. Scott had suggested should be increased to three.

Rette was grateful to them for their lenience. Her other grades had always been high, and they seemed to sense that the fact that algebra had proved a stumbling block put Loretta to shame. When Jeff appeared, they treated him with casual courtesy and made it as easy for Rette as possible. Rette repaid them by getting down to the most serious work of her entire school career.

Somewhere she found the courage to confess the unvarnished truth to Jeff. She went back with him practically to the beginning of the algebra book and started over, refusing to leave a theorem or an illustration until she thoroughly understood the problem involved.

She was a slow pupil. Added to the discomfiture of Jeff's mere presence was a natural ineptitude for figures that was hard to conquer. But Rette tried.

And Jeff, she had to admit after only the second lesson, was a good and a remarkably patient tutor. He didn't patronize her, as she had feared. He didn't even seem to think of her as a person. She was simply his job, and he came in on time each tutoring night and promptly got down to work.

When Cathy and Judy and the rest of the girls found that she had Jeff as a tutor, Rette was afraid they might ridicule her or tease her, and she prepared herself for such a contingency with an iron front. But, instead, they seemed to feel she was lucky. She even went up a notch or two in Judy's estimation.

"Gosh," she exclaimed enviously, "what a swell break!"

Tony happened to be out on the first two nights Jeff

came to the house, but on the Tuesday following the two boys met.

Jeff had out his hand to Rette's brother with unconcealed admiration. "I'm proud to know you," he said, and he meant it. Sincerity shone in his eyes.

Tony always belittled his war record, but he was willing enough to talk about the boys he had fought with in the 82d, and Jeff had a cousin who had been a paratrooper, whom Tony had known well. For the first time Jeff loitered after the hour's lesson was over, chatting with Tony and Mrs. Larkin until after nine o'clock.

Rette, though she was left on the side lines, was proud of her family. Tony was quite a guy to have for a brother, and her mother, as usual, was attractive and gay. Jeff liked her mother, she could tell. All the boys liked Mrs. Larkin, all Tony's friends. She made them feel important and interesting. Rette could never quite discover how she managed it, but she did.

After Jeff had left, Rette told Tony, "That's the fellow who will probably get the flying prize."

Tony raised interested eyebrows. "So! He seems like a darn good kid."

From Tony this was high praise, and Rette unconsciously basked in reflected glory. "He knows more about airplanes!" she said. "He can spot the different makes the way some kids can tell all the cars."

Tony laughed. "That's not unusual, Rette, for a boy."

But Rette was still impressed.

The date for the announcement of the essay contest winner was set for April 1, with adult disregard for the fact that it was also April Fools' Day. Mr. Irish was scheduled to make the presentation of the award in assembly, and Rette couldn't seem to keep her stomach from churning as she walked to school.

It wasn't that she thought she had a chance of winning

herself. She was sure that the submission of the second essay had fixed that for keeps. But she knew, from his tension during the hour they had spent together the night before, how much the prize would mean to Jeff Chandler.

Jeff had even admitted it, when she questioned him. "Sure, I'd give my eyeteeth to learn to fly," he said. "But then, so would a lot of other guys. And gals," he added belatedly.

"You know, Rette," he said a little later, "the people who win prizes are never the people you'd expect. Wait till Commencement. I bet you'll see. The kids who get ahead are the last ones you'd pick, and a good many of the high-school hot shots just never amount to a hill of beans."

He's trying to talk himself out of being too hopeful, Rette thought. She smiled gently and didn't argue the point, but in the morning she was almost as excited for Jeff as she would have been had she nurtured any expectations herself.

Among the pupils gathering in Rette's home room when she arrived, the usual wags were clowning and the practical jokers were out in full force. There were seniors who, belying their years and sophistication, still considered it funny to put tacks on the teacher's desk chair. There was the inevitable wit who stuffed crumpled newspaper into a girl's desk and took great delight in hiding her books.

On Margaret's desk was a note, not too subtle, asking her to call Mrs. Taxies at lunch time, and giving the telephone number of the station cabstand. Rette herself found a note that read, "Please see Mr. Martin in his office immediately." She wadded it into a ball with a knowing smile and fired it into the wastebasket at the front of the room.

Jeff Chandler came in rather late, looking very debonair. He went right over to Elise's desk, where he stayed talking until the bell for assembly rang.

As he went out of the room in front of her, Rette couldn't help following him secretly with her eyes. She admired his apparent unconcern, when he had every cause to appear anxious. What she wouldn't give to have that kind of poise, to be able to look self-possessed in such a time of crisis! Her heart was fluttering like a captive pigeon right now.

Many eyes, inevitably, were on the seniors, as the lowerclassmen speculated and wished that they too had turned sixteen. The appearance of Mr. Irish again created a ripple of excitement among the girls. He seemed not unaware of it, Rette thought. Perhaps no man was above the flattery of feminine applause.

At the beginning of assembly there were the usual lengthy preliminaries. The orchestra played with rather disorganized exuberance, and Mr. Martin made announcements that seemed exceptionally dull.

Finally, however, he came to the point.

"I know that you are awaiting with interest the announcement that Mr. Irish is here to make. Let me first say that the committee of judges considered all of forty-nine essays." He turned to the young man behind him. "So there are forty-nine potential flyers in our midst." Then he continued, redundantly: "Many of the compositions were of high quality. Three were indeed outstanding. The judges did not have an easy time."

Rette's fingers were cold, but the palms of her hands were perspiring. She could just see the back of Jeff Chandler's head three rows in front of where she sat. It was unwavering, and she wondered how he felt beneath such superficial calmness. She swallowed hard.

Stephen Irish was on his feet now, nodding his head briefly in response to Mr. Martin's introduction. He held an envelope in his hand, and as he walked forward he tapped it against his left wrist as though he found himself unexpectedly nervous.

"In behalf of Wings Airport," he said with formality, "it gives me great pleasure to award this prize to a student of Avondale High. At your Commencement in June I hope to be able to make a second award to this same student—" he paused and grinned, "a special Wings Airport diploma for a solo flight."

He glanced momentarily at the envelope in his hand, then back at the assembly. "The prize of a one-hundred-dollar block of flying lessons goes to Loretta Larkin," he said.

Rette sat as though her stomach were caught in a vise. She heard the short gasp of surprise that swept the auditorium, then the conventional applause—not so loud as it would have been for a school hero like Jeff Chandler, but loud enough.

There must be a mistake, she thought, if she thought at all. The echo of her own name rang in her ears like an April-fool joke. She had given up all hopes of the prize so completely that she couldn't believe it was true.

But Margaret was nudging her in the side and Judy was thumping her on the back. "Go on up and get it," Judy whispered. "Go on!"

Rette couldn't have moved at that moment had she been threatened by fire or flood, and fortunately Mr. Irish gave her a chance to collect her scattered wits.

"Before Miss Larkin comes forward," he said, "I'd like you all to know that the judges chose her particular essay for one special reason. It is one of the most completely natural pieces of teen-age writing that any of us has ever read. And I think that I'm safe in saying that you'll have a chance to see what I'm talking about in a coming issue of the *Arrow*."

He turned slightly toward the principal, who nodded, then back to the students. "And now, Miss Larkin—" The envelope looked very white in his hand.

Somehow Rette reached the center aisle, pushed and prodded helpfully by her intervening classmates, over whose knees she had to stumble before she could stand alone. Doggedly she advanced toward the outstretched envelope, which was beginning to swim before her eyes. Rette wasn't unaccustomed to the limelight, but always before she had been one of a team when she had starred. Now she was utterly, alarmingly, *entirely*, by herself.

She felt, as she accepted the prize with an almost inaudible "Thank you," that she was incapable of finesse. So overwhelmed that she couldn't even manage a convincing smile, she took the envelope and fled back to her seat under the cover of repeated applause.

On the way, for one vivid second, she saw Jeff Chandler's face. He was clapping with enthusiam, and smiling his congratulations in the most sportsmanlike manner, but in his eyes Rette detected disappointment that was naked and unashamed.

CHAPTER ELEVEN

Rette had never before walked in glory.

Her progress from the auditorium back to her home room was like a triumphal march. Everybody had to congratulate her, the boys tongue-in-the-cheek because they were surprised and rather shocked that a *girl* had won, but the girls with superior pride.

Rette scarcely knew what she said in reply to the deluge of felicitations. She was almost glad when Miss Kennedy, Mr. Martin's secretary, rescued her by coming to her home room to stay that Mr. Irish would like to speak with her in the office before he left the school.

She trotted along in Miss Kennedy's wake with her heart still beating like a trip hammer, feeling proud and humble at the same time, emotionally all mixed up.

The principal of the school and the flyer were standing just within the door of Mr. Martin's private office. They turned when Rette entered, and Stephen Irish grinned at her apparent confusion.

"Kind of surprised you, eh?" Mr. Martin said.

"Surprised!"

"We tried to let you know just before assembly, so that you could be prepared. Didn't you get a note?"

Rette's eyes widened, remembering. "I thought it was an April-fool stunt," she gasped.

Mr. Irish really laughed now. He sat on the corner of the principal's desk and slapped his knee while he exchanged a glance with Mr. Martin. Then he said to Loretta, "When do you want to start?"

"Start—flying?" Rette couldn't believe that all this luck was real.

"Sure."

"Why, I don't know. I hadn't thought—"

"What about tomorrow morning—if Saturday's a good day for you? Otherwise we can schedule your lessons for weekdays, after school. Be sure you have your parents' permission first, too."

"Tomorrow morning's fine," Rette gathered her wits to say, and they made an appointment for eleven o'clock. "And I do want to thank you," she added, remembering her manners. "I'm still sort of—knocked for a loop."

Then, beating a hasty retreat, she wondered why she couldn't have expressed herself in a manner less slangy. "Tomboy, tomboy, tomboy," she muttered to herself between her teeth.

Loretta lived through the rest of the day in a daze. She was glad it was Friday, because even the teachers seemed to relax on the last day of the school week. The faculty members in whose classes she sat smiled at her with understanding, and few of them asked her to recite.

At noon Rette wanted to call her mother to tell her the marvelous news, but the phone was so public, right in the anteroom of Mr. Martin's office, that she decided to resist the impulse and wait until she could see her face to face.

Of all the girls, Elise seemed to be the most impressed.

"I should think you'd be so thrilled!" she cried with excite-ment. "I'm positively green with envy. When do you start?"

"Tomorrow morning," Rette told her, feeling almost embarrassed by such huge good fortune.

"Oh, pooh!" Elise said, pushing her pretty lower lip forward in a pout. "I'd come watch you take off, but I've got to be at the gym, decorating, on account of the Ball."

Rette had completely forgotten that the next day was the Saturday of the Senior Ball. For nearly a whole day she had forgotten, and to be reminded of it now took just a bit of the edge from her unexpected success.

Then she rallied and replied: "Oh, but I doubt if I'll actually get a chance to go up, my first lesson! I don't think there will be anything to *see*."

But Rette was wrong. The next morning, when she timidly presented herself to Mr. Irish at the airport office, he told her that both an instructor and a plane were ready.

"I'm letting you have a Cessna," he said as though this were quite a privilege. "In a Cessna instructor and pupil sit side by side, where in a Piper Cub you'd have to sort of crane your neck to see the instrument panel."

Rette drew herself up to her full five feet four, because it seemed to her that Mr. Irish had implied that she was short. "You mean," she asked, trying not to sound too ex-cited, "I'm to go up—today?"

"Sure. You've won the prize—you've got your Dad's OK. The only way to learn to ride a horse is to get on it." Stephen Irish grinned.

"For you, Mr. Irish," a girl holding a telephone re-ceiver in her hand called from an inner office, and while Rette stood waiting for her sponsor to return she realized that her hands had turned clammy with agitation. It seemed to her that everything was happening too fast.

It wasn't that she'd lost her nerve or anything like that. It was just that she felt like such a greenhorn. Why, she didn't even have the foggiest notion of how an airplane worked, what kept it up—anything! She hoped she'd draw an instructor who wouldn't expect too much.

Because Mr. Irish was by now familiar to her, she wished he were teaching her—she'd have confidence in him; but he had told her that he was so busy with managing operations that he no longer had much time to instruct. With blue April skies after a rainy, blowy March, business at the new airport had increased by leaps and bounds. From mechanics to executives, everybody about the place looked busy and intent.

Mr. Irish banged the telephone into its cradle and called to Rette, "Be right back," as he strode from the room. In a few minutes he returned, talking to a slender girl in slacks who walked confidently along by his side.

The girl was about Tony's age, Rette could see as they came toward her. She had shoulder-length brown hair which curled at the ends, and her brown eyes had golden flecks in them. Her mouth was rather large, with a merry quirk to the corners. She looked pleasant and assured.

"Loretta Larkin—Pat Creatore." Mr. Irish introduced them, using their first names.

Pat held out her hand. "Glad to know you. Congratulations on winning that prize."

Rette murmured, "Thanks," astonished that the news had spread. She wondered why Mr. Irish had brought the girl over, and was just ready to ask, "Are you taking flying lessons too?" when he told her.

"Pat's going to be your instructor." He winked at Rette solemnly. "And you can take my word for it, she really is good!"

"But tough," Pat added with a purely feminine inflection. She had gathered her long hair into her hands and was securing it at the back of her neck with a big tortoise-shell barrette.

Rette couldn't keep astonishment out of her eyes. It had never occurred to her that she might have a girl for an instructor, yet when she stopped to consider it—why not?

Pat, sensing her reaction, looked at Mr. Irish and laughed. For Rette's further enlightenment the airport manager added: "Pat taught the father of one of your classmates to fly, couple of years ago. Carter Wynn."

"Elise's father?"

"Not here," Pat said. "Over at Wyndham, before this airport was built." She glanced at her watch, turned to the desk that flanked the front office, and asked Rette to sign her name to a charge slip that looked not unlike a department store sales slip. It bore the date, a ship number, the instructor's name, and Rette's address, as well as the take-off time.

"All right. Let's get going," she said.

Rette followed Pat down the steps of the converted farmhouse and across a stretch of grass just tinged with spring chartreuse. Three small planes were lined up in a row, and Pat went to the middle one and inspected the wooden chocks under the wheels.

"Ever flown before?" she asked Rette.

"Just once, in an air liner," Rette said. She was looking at the little plane with curiosity. "This seems so small!"

Pat nodded. "Small planes are a lot more fun!"

She opened the door of the cockpit and took out a couple of seat cushions, tossing them on the ground. "Let's sit down for a few minutes before we climb in."

Obediently, Rette sat down.

Pat gathered her knees in her arms and asked casually, "D'you understand what makes an airplane fly?"

"I think," said Rette, "that it stays up because the wings push the air down."

"Not bad," said Pat, and she started to talk about the theory of flying. "Get rid of the idea that a plane is only an air-going sort of automobile," she told Rette. "It isn't. Nor is flying easy to learn, as you've probably been told. Flying is done largely with the imagination. Your acts are going to be based on a mental image of the airplane, its controls and maneuvers, and it's important that you get that image straight."

Rette tried her best to follow this pretty girl sitting opposite her as she described the parts of an airplane, the way in which it flies. Some of what Pat said she could comprehend, but not all of it. The vocabulary of flying was strange and therefore rather alarming. She was relieved when Pat said, "I don't want to overwhelm you," and jumped up. "Let's get in."

She put a foot on the metal step and climbed into the cabin from the right side while Rette got in from the left. Pat showed her new pupil how to fasten her seat belt, then explained the ground check of the instrument panel and controls necessary before every take-off. Rette listened carefully with her hand on the little wheel that Pat called the "stick."

"The controls are very simple," the instructor explained. "For straight and level flight the rudder pedals and control stick are neutral. When you move the stick forward, the elevators on the tail go down. This raises the tail and causes the plane to nose down. When you pull the stick back toward you, the elevators go up, and the plane climbs."

Rette tried to fix it in her mind. *Back on the stick to*

climb, forward to nose down. It seemed that there was a good deal to remember.

But that wasn't all. The action of the ailerons on the wings had to be explained, and the use of the rudder pedals.

"All right, let's go," Pat said finally, and showed Rette how to start the engine.

The plane had a self-starter, and in no time they were taxiing in S-turns toward the runway. "We always take off and land into the wind," Pat said as they zigzagged along. "Keep your hand on the stick *lightly*—rest your feet *lightly* on the pedals—and follow me through on the controls."

Rette tried to do as she was told. Under Pat's expert guidance the plane was turning into position for the take-off and the engine was beginning to roar with increased power as the throttle was advanced.

"Now just relax," Pat said, turning to the younger girl with a smile. "*Relax,* I said! You've got a death grip on that stick!"

Rette hadn't realized that she was holding on to the wheel for dear life. The palm of her hand was damp with sweat, and as she tried to loosen up and settle back in her seat she realized that her back was so tense that it ached.

"That's better," Pat grinned, turning to meet Rette's eyes. "All right, here we go. Just follow through on the controls until you get used to being in the air."

Pat peered to the right and left and into the air ahead of the ship, then made her clearing turn preparatory to take off. "All clear," she murmured as, with her left hand, she eased the throttle ahead. The plane started rolling down the runway, over the rather rough terrain that had grown the Tisdale's corn only last year or the year before.

Faster . . . faster . . . faster! Rette realized that they were in the air only because there were no more bumps. She glanced out of the cockpit window and saw the airport buildings drifting away below them. As the hangar receded into the distance, Rette's qualms receded too. She wriggled back in her seat happily, really relaxed now, and looked down at the beautiful pattern of green and brown fields. Then she turned to Pat.

"This is such fun!" she cried.

But Pat Creatore didn't give Rette long simply to enjoy the view. "You take over the controls now," she called above the steady drone of the engine. "Just keep the plane flying along straight and level, as it is now."

It was astonishing, Rette found, what a light movement of stick or rudder was needed to control the plane. Compared with steering a bicycle, this required a featherweight touch.

Finally the instructor said: "I'll take it now. We'll climb a bit. Then you can try some simple turns."

Rette sat back and looked down at the earth beneath the plane. Strangely enough, she experienced no sensation of height at all. Houses and fields and ribbonlike highways seemed smaller, to be sure. But looking at them from the cabin of the plane seemed not unlike looking at the countryside from the window of a moving car. It was just a *different* view, Rette thought, and was reminded of looking down on a Christmas-tree village, with the cows and people like figures from Lilliput, too tiny to be real.

Now the cars moving on highways were beetles, and the altimeter needle was moving up past the nine-hundred-foot mark. At one thousand feet Pat leveled off and said, "Follow me through on a left turn now."

Rette held the stick with one hand and let her feet

rest on the rudder pedals very lightly, so that she could feel the delicacy with which Pat turned the wheel and pushed on the left rudder.

"Left rudder, left stick," she was saying as the tip of the left wing dropped below the horizon, showing blue sky under the right wing as the plane banked. "Neutralize."

Rette felt the controls return to neutral, yet the plane kept on turning. It was a little confusing. "To roll out of a turn," Pat said, "apply opposite stick and rudder." She suited her actions to words, and the plane began to fly straight and level once more.

"Now you try it," Pat said. "Left turn."

Rette tried to copy her instructor's handling of the left stick and left rudder, and the left wing dropped suddenly down—'way down! Looking out of the cabin window at the earth, a thousand feet below, Rette had the sensation of lying on her side and floating over the fields and woods.

"Gently!" Pat shouted. "Gently! You act like a boy, yanking the controls around like that. Easy does it."

Rette felt the stick and rudder move as Pat took over and quite effortlessly resumed level flight.

"Now try it again."

This time Rette, embarrassed by the rebuke, was *too* gentle, but on the third turn she did better, except that the nose of the plane exhibited a persistent tendency to pull up. Then, at Pat's command, she tried some right turns, with variable results. She could feel herself growing weary from the effort of remembering so many things at once, but Pat seemed unaware of it.

"Another right turn now," she called.

This time Rette succeeded in keeping the nose down, but her rudder pressure was so light that the plane slipped into its turn. She looked at Pat questioningly. Even with her lack of experience she knew that the turn didn't feel right.

Pat explained. "There's an expression called 'flying by the seat of your pants,'" she said. "Know what I mean?"

Rette nodded. "The way you bank with a bicycle when you're going around a curve?"

Pat smiled. "That's right." Then, suddenly, she said: "That's enough for today. Look down and tell me where the airport is."

Rette peered down on the tidy world so far below, but could see nothing in the least familiar.

"I haven't the slightest idea where we are!" she cried.

Pat smiled, and pointed out some landmarks, explaining how to get a sense of location from the air. She turned the plane toward home, and Rette could feel a gradual loss of altitude as they came in to circle the field in a glide.

To Rette, as they approached the runway, the plane seemed to be going very fast. Then she could feel Pat move the stick back, more and more, until the wheels touched the field in a three-point landing. They were back on the ground again.

Rette knew, for the first time in her life, what it was like to be weak with excitement. When she unfastened her safety belt and climbed out of the plane, her knees felt wobbly and she had the sensation of stepping too high, as though she had just climbed down off a horse.

Her mouth was dry and she was perspiring, her dungarees clinging to the backs of her legs. But she was filled with pentup exhilaration. She had made her first flight—she had actually handled the controls of a plane—and it was even more fun than she had dreamed!

For just a second she glanced back at the trainer, lined

up neatly between two other ships. *My* plane, she thought possessively. It looked very bright and trim.

At Pat's behest, before she left the airport, Loretta bought a flight log, a little oblong book in which a record of her time in the air would be kept.

Pat entered the time of the first flight—thirty-five minutes—and signed it. Rette looked at the entry proudly. Her first thirty-five minutes of dual instruction! It seemed incredible to conceive that by the time her ten hours of lessons were finished, she might be abel to take the plane up in the air *alone!*

CHAPTER TWELVE

It seemed anticlimactic to ride a bike away from a flying lesson, but Rette was feeling so buoyant that it tickled her sense of humor. From sheer high spirits she sang the refrain of a Hit Parade song as she rode back toward town.

The country road was empty along the margin of the airport's new wire fence. Rette kept glancing back at the hangar as she pedaled along, and when she reached a small copse of trees that blotted it out for a moment she stood up and raced with the wind until the building came into view again. The knowledge that she'd be coming back here time after time was sweet and fresh. She felt as though she'd been given the key to a wonderful city. As though she *belonged*.

It was a feeling Rette had always craved, and had never quite achieved in high school. In athletics sometimes, working with a team, but never socially, had Rette felt quite at home. Out here at Wings, Rette was sure she could fit in. Out here the standards were adult and therefore less inflexible than the pattern to which she was expected to conform at school.

" 'With a hey-nonny-nonny and a hot-cha-cha!' "

Rette had to yell; she had to bounce up and down on her bicycle seat; she was overflowing with exuberance, and she had to spill some of her excitement or burst.

"So you had fun!"

From the same spot long the airport fence where she had met him on that other Saturday came Jeff Chandler's voice. Embarrassed that he had caught her acting like a youngster, Rette tried to cover her confusion with a flip retort.

"Swell fun, but isn't this where I came in?"

Jeff laughed, bearing no malice. "Are my eyes green?" he asked. "They should be."

Suddenly Rette was contrite. "I'm sorry, Jeff. I wish it could have been both of us."

"Tell me about it," Jeff said. "I saw you land. At least I think it was you. In a Cessna 120. Right?"

"Right!" Rette's eyes glowed, and she began to forget herself. "It's difficult, Jeff, different from anything else in the world. I wish I could explain—"

She found herself talking without restraint, because Jeff was really interested. He wasn't just asking questions out of courtesy. He was as avid as she.

It was wonderful, in her present mood, to have a good listener. Rette forgot that Jeff was one of the most popular boys in high school. She talked to him without self-consciousness, her words tumbling one over the other, her natural enthusiasm bubbling up like a spring.

She dropped her bike on the grass and leaned against the fence and watched planes take off and come in, still talking about flying. Jeff talked too now. He knew things about airplanes, technical things, that were beyond Rette's comprehension but still interesting to her. They chattered away like fast friends.

Finally Jeff glanced at his wrist watch, then whistled. "It's lunch time," he said. "I thought I was getting hungry. Better be starting back to town."

"My family will think I've crashed," Rette giggled as

she picked up her bike. "Mother was all hepped up about feminine equality until I won the prize, but since yesterday she's been treating me the way she treated Tony before he went off to the wars. As though I might never come back."

Jeff chuckled. "What about Tony? Was he surprised?"

"He doesn't know about the prize yet. He's been off on a business trip since Thursday, but he's getting home today."

"And Gramp?"

"Pleased as Punch!" Rette said. "And a little jealous, I think. He's afraid I won't have enough time for our pinochle games."

They rode along in silence for a few minutes. Then Rette said: "Dad's not too keen about it all. I guess he thinks that one flyer in a family is enough."

A truck roared toward them, and Rette and Jeff separated, one hugging the grass on one side of the macadam road, one on the other. When they met again the first houses of Avondale were in sight, and somehow the spell of the morning was broken. Rette was aware that her short hair was wind-whipped and untidy, and Jeff seemed in a hurry to get home.

At the turn into Cherry Tree Road, Rette would have muttered a " 'By now," and ridden off without stopping, but Jeff halted her with an unexpected question.

"Who're you going to the dance with tonight?" he asked.

There was no way to dodge out of a clean admission. "I'm not going," Rette told him, trying not to sound sullen. Gone was the exhilaration of the past hour. Her heart began to hammer and she felt as though, just on the verge of escape, she had fallen into a trap.

"Not going?" Jeff was incredulous. "Oh, now say!" He

braked, and his feet sawed the ground as he slipped off the seat of his bike.

Rette didn't reply. She wanted to get away, but she didn't know how to do it. With acute personal torture she waited for his next remark.

"But you can't do that! *Everybody's* going to be there. And after winning a prize and all."

Belligerence—Rette's old defense—crept into her voice. "This is a free country," she said. "I don't have to go if I don't want to." Why can't he *see,* she wondered? Why can't he let me alone? She could almost hear the beat of her heart now; she could feel its overwrought pounding. Every additional word she said made her more unattractive and she knew it. But she couldn't seem to help herself.

Jeff still didn't understand. With masculine impenetrability he heard only her words, not suspecting the secret they were covering. "You ought to be ashamed!" he shot back. "Where's your school spirit, anyway?"

Rette could feel tears of anger and frustration sting her eyelids. She kept her head lowered, so that Jeff wouldn't see, and then, appallingly, a tear slipped over and slid down her cheek. Quick as a flash she turned, ready to mount her bike and ride off, no matter what impression she might leave behind her.

But Jeff had seen. Rette heard the crash of his bicycle as he dropped it against the curb. In a second he was at her side.

"Why heck!" he said. "Why, heck, I didn't mean to hurt your feelings! Gee, Rette! Why, gee whiz!"

Awkwardly, he patted her on the back, and because he was contrite and sympathetic Rette was still further unnerved.

"I—I don't think you're being fair," she choked.

"But you said—"

Then suddenly a great light seemed to dawn for Jeff. He hesitated and, without finishing the sentence, dropped his hand. "Look," he said, without meaning to add insult to injury, "why don't you ride over to school with Elise and me?"

Nothing could have dried Rette's tears more quickly. In the most scathing tone she could muster she said, "Don't be ridiculous.". Then, without a backward glance, she rode off.

It was hard to regain her self-possession in the two blocks that lay between the corner where she had left Jeff and her home. The family would be eagerly awaiting news of her flying lesson, and she had to be ready to satisfy them. But the spontaneous enthusiasm with which she would have burst into the house was gone now. It would be an effort to put up a front.

She put her bike away properly in the garage, instead of dropping it by the driveway in her usual headlong fashion. Fearing that traces of tears still showed, she gave herself as much time as possible before she ran up the back steps to the kitchen door.

She needn't have taken such pains. Far from being the center of attention, Rette came into the house practically unnoticed. Her mother, in a flowered chambray apron, was tenderly sliding a freshly baked layer of cake onto a wire rack, and Tony was helping Ellen Alden make sandwiches, which seemed to be amusing Mr. Larkin, who was leaning against the doorjamb with a pipe in his mouth.

Tony looked up and saw Loretta and said immediately: "Here, Small Fry, you take over. I'm no good at this sort of thing."

Mrs. Larkin said, "Hello, dear," abstractedly as she bent to take a second layer of the cake from the oven, and Rette's dad simply grinned and waved his pipe. "Your brother," he said, "acts as though a bread knife were a grass whip. Look at those slices, will you? Just look."

Rette's first reaction was to be offended at this lack of interest on her family's part in her morning's adventure. Then she remembered that she had told her mother and dad that she didn't expect to go up in the air for her first lesson. She took over Tony's job with assumed casualness, and only after the sandwiches were spread and the crusts cut off did she say, as though in passing. "By the way, Tony, did Mother tell you about the prize?"

"Darling!" Mrs. Larkin was repentant. "Tony and Ellen just blew in, and I was so busy with this cake I forgot." She turned to her son. "Rette won the essay contest—you know the one—and we're all just puffed up with pride."

"Rette! Wonderful!" It was Ellen speaking, before Tony could say, "Gee, that's swell!" The older girl put her arm around Loretta's shoulders in a spontaneous hug of approval. Her eyes were bright with congratulation. "And you're actually going to take flying lessons? Aren't you simply thrilled?"

"Flying lessons?" Tony's eyebrows shot up.

Mrs. Larkin flicked a pot holder against her son's shoulder. "You never really listen any more," she accused him, then glanced slyly at Ellen, who was suddenly absorbed in arranging the sandwiches on a plate. "The prize is a hundred-dollar block of flying lessons. Isn't that something, for a girl sixteen?"

"Well, say!" Tony's surprise was evident. "It sure is!" He looked at Rette as though he were seeing her through new eyes. "When do you start, kid?"

Rette said with dignity, "I have started, this morning."

At the same time a tremor seemed to pass across Mrs. Larkin's shoulders. "I'm not sure I'm going to like it, when she actually gets in the air."

"I went up today," Rette said, "in a Cessna. It was fun."

The understatement had the effect of rocking the family back on its several heels.

"You went *up?*" Mrs. Larkin squealed. "Well, why didn't you tell us? For heaven's sake!"

Rette's dad chuckled. "She hasn't had a chance." Then, his voice holding a slight trace of anxiety, he asked quickly, "Was Mr. Irish along?"

Loretta shook her head. "No. My instructor's a girl. Pat Creatore, her name is."

"I've heard of her!" Ellen said. "She was a Wasp—a ferry-command pilot, I think."

"That's right," Rette was able to say. "She's had almost three thousand hours in the air."

"Three thousand hours?" Mrs. Larkin asked. "Is it possible?"

"Even probable," Tony replied. "Some of the gals really piled 'em up."

Almost shyly Ellen asked Rette, "Was it as exciting as you'd hoped?"

"Exciting?" Rette pondered. Could that sweeping elation be called excitement? "I don't know—It's entirely different from anything I've ever done. And I was so *busy!*" she added. "I've never been so busy in my life."

Tony laughed out loud. "You'll get over that," he told her in big-brotherly fashion, "when the newness has worn off." He picked up the plate of sandwiches and carried it in to the dining-room table as Ellen filled some glasses with milk and Mrs. Larkin started to ladle cream of tomato soup into white ironstone plates.

"Will you get the bowl of salad out of the refrigerator, Rette?"

One minute she was soaring through space, and the next she was obeying mundane instructions from her mother. Rette marveled at the complication of her life and wondered if Tony ever felt like two persons, instead of one.

She carried the bowl in to the table, pulled up chairs, and sorted through the silver box to find the salad set, just as though it were the most natural thing in the world, but every gesture seemed to her astonishing and separate, and she couldn't tell which was the real world, which the dream. She smiled at Ellen vaguely, bit into a sandwich, and said, "Mmm. Good!"

It was while they were all still sitting at the lunch table that the phone rang. Tony, who was nearest the dining-room door, answered, and called, "Rette!"

"Who is it?" Rette asked as she scraped back her chair.

"I don't know. A girl."

Of course it would be a girl. That went without saying. Rette blamed herself for a ridiculous and quickly stilled flutter of her heart. She went to the telephone, said, "Hello," rather stolidly and then added, in some surprise, "Oh, Elise?"

"How did you like your flying lesson?" Elise asked.

"It was fun!" Rette told her, without attempting to convey the impossible.

"I'll bet! I want to hear all about it, but just now I'm in a tear."

That was nothing new. Elise was always in a tear, and Rette couldn't help wondering whether she really did want to hear, or whether she was just saying so. But the thought was just a flash, here and gone, because Elise was racing on.

"What I really called about was tonight. I wanted to know if you wouldn't go over to the gym early with Jeff and Larry Carpenter and me. We're renting a juke box, you know, and there's that to see to, and Dora was going to take tickets but she's in bed with the grippe and I thought maybe you'd fill in for her. I really need some help."

Her voice was so light and breathless over the wire that

111

Rette had to listen carefully to catch every word, but gradually it dawned upon her that Elise, with admirable tact, was offering her a chance to go to the Senior Ball in Dora's place and at the same time to save face by having a job to do. It would practically amount to a double date with Larry and Elise and Jeff. She wondered how much Jeff had had to do with this proposal and bit her lip, ready to flare up angrily at the mere possibility of being patronized.

But Elise was hurrying on, still breathlessly, giving Rette no chance to refuse. "We'll stop by for you about seven thirty if that's all right. 'By now. I've really *got* to run."

Rette was torn by conflicting emotions. On the one hand she was ashamed and embarrassed that Jeff must have interceded in her behalf; on the other hand her heart leaped at the thought of appearing at the party in her new guise as student pilot. She was aware that she had become, overnight, a kind of public figure in the eyes of the senior class, and that failure to appear would invite inevitable Monday-morning questions to which she had no convincing answers. She couldn't just blurt out the truth: "I didn't come to the party because I didn't have a date."

In a split second, now, she had to decide what course to follow, whether to accept the cover of Elise's fabrication, or whether to refuse the indignity of playing second fiddle to Dora Phillips and stick to her original contention that she considered class parties "dumb."

Weakly, she heard herself saying into the mouthpiece: "All right. I'll be glad to help out if I can." Then she put the receiver back into the cradle gently, making no noise, and stood by the telephone half despising herself for such frailty, half pleased that she would be going to the dance under the sponsorship of such a popular group.

The sound of repartee floated in from the dining room, followed by Mrs. Larkin's lighthearted laugh. I'll have to press my plaid taffeta, Rette was thinking, and wash my hair. She glanced at her nails for the first time in days and frowned. She'd need a manicure too. Then she looked at the clock. It was already two thirty. The afternoon would be too short for all she had to do.

Walking back to the dining room, to slip inconspicuously into her place, she couldn't help wishing that she had a new dress. Practically all the girls got new frocks for the Senior Ball. Still, the taffeta wasn't too bad. It had a low, round neck and the shortest of puffed sleeves, and the skirt was simply yards around. With Grandmother's cameo locket strung on a velvet ribbon to set off the neckline—Rette reached for the last sandwich on the plate automatically and began to plan.

CHAPTER THIRTEEN

There's no doubt about it, Rette decided as she stood before the mirror on the door of her bedroom closet, a long skirt certainly does something for a girl.

She turned, and the skirt swished. She glanced over her shoulder, admiring its sweep. Then, in the mirror, she saw Gramp's reflection. He was standing in the doorway, swaying back and forth on his heels, his hands behind him.

"You look a great deal like your grandmother," he said.

Rette knew that he was paying her a supreme compliment. In Gramp's eyes there had never been a girl so beautiful, never would be. There was something in the way the old man stood there, looking at her, that made Rette's throat tighten and her eyes smart. She ran to him and threw her arms impulsively around his neck.

"You're sweet," she said.

Gramp held her off and looked at her again. "It's a relief," he said, changing his tone abruptly, "to see you in decent clothes for a change." His nose wrinkled. "Those pants you wear—"

Rette giggled. "They're called bluejeans."

She went back to the mirror and repaired any possible damage to the powder on her nose. Once more she ran a comb through her short hair, and once more wished it were long—shoulder-length like Elise's, and blonde instead of brown.

Under her grandfather's admiring scrutiny, however, she felt attractive, and certainly more self-confident than usual.

"You'll be the belle of the ball," Gramp said.

Rette laughed. "Hardly that." If she sounded cynical she had good reason, Loretta thought, considering the number of parties she had suffered through. All she hoped for the evening was that, due to the winning of the flying prize, she would not be too obviously neglected. Taking tickets would help fill in time until the dance was well under way. Then maybe everybody would be too busy to notice whether she stood on the side lines or repaired to the locker room more often than most.

Downstairs the doorbell pealed, and Rette grabbed her coat off the bed. She had butterflies in her tummy in earnest now. She was more nervous than when she had stepped into the Cessna and buckled her safety belt, but in a different way.

Both Jeff and Larry were standing in the living room, self-conscious and a little abashed, as in Rette's experience boys always were before a party. Mrs. Larkin was valiantly making conversation when her daughter came down the stairs, but even her best efforts were unappreciated tonight.

Rette was afraid that Larry might be resentful of the part he was unexpectedly playing. He was a tall boy, thin and fair-haired, with the reputation of being sophisticated, and she was consequently afraid of him. She didn't meet his eyes as she murmured: " 'Lo, Jeff. Hello, Larry," trying to keep her voice as light as her mother's and overcome the tendency to sound gruff and boyish.

"Hi," Jeff greeted her hurriedly, while Larry jerked his head and muttered something unintelligible. "All set?

We've got to get going. Work to do!" He turned to Mrs. Larkin. "You'll excuse us?"

"Of course." Always gracious, Mrs. Larkin waved them off, standing in the doorway and calling, "Have a good time!"

Rette glanced back at her mother as at a safe haven. She experienced a moment of panic, when she wanted to bolt back to her room. But somehow she was at the door of the Carpenters' shiny new Pontiac, and Jeff was handing her in one side while Larry crawled under the wheel on the other. Wedged between the two boys, Rette felt almost protected. She tried to settle back easily, as she'd watched other girls do. Larry turned, and started back down Cherry Tree Road toward the Wynns'.

"Hear you've been up in the air already," he said.

Rette's first flying lesson furnished a safe and interesting topic of conversation all the way to Elise's house. Jeff guided the talk, but Rette hurried obediently along the roads he opened, feeling her tension slacken as he put her more and more at ease.

"Shall I wait in the car?" she asked as Larry pulled into the Wynns' drive.

"Better come along in," Jeff advised. "If Elise is ready, it'll be the first time. When it comes to dressing for a party she's a poke."

Upstairs and down, the Wynn house was ablaze with light. It was Mr. Wynn who opened the door to Jeff's knock, saying, "Come in, come in," as though he were annoyed at something, and standing back so that they could all troop into the broad center hall.

Apparently it wasn't only Elise who was dressing to go out, because Mr. Wynn was in a tuxedo, cut with precision to fit his short, stocky frame. Keen blue eyes inspected Loretta candidly. "You're George Larkin's daughter, aren't you?" he asked.

Rette remembered that once before, on one of their very occasional meetings, he had greeted her with the same remark, apparently seeing in Rette a strong family resemblance to her dad.

"Yes, I am," Rette said.

"Read in the paper you'd won the flying prize Elise has been talking about. Congratulations."

"Thanks." Rette hadn't known that a notice had appeared in the newspaper, but to hear of it made her feel important. She mustered enough self-assurance to say to Mr. Wynn, "A girl you know is my instructor—Pat Creatore."

Unexpectedly Mr. Wynn's right hand shot out and slapped Rette vigorously on the shoulder. "Best doggone instructor on the Atlantic seaboard, Patty is!" he cried. Then, as though this clinched the matter, "She taught me."

"I know." Rette couldn't help grinning at his enthusiasm. "She told me."

"You like her?" Mr. Wynn asked while the boys waited.

"Very much."

"Sure!" Elise's father approved. "She's a great girl." Then his sharp eyes narrowed and he seemed to be thinking. "The men in charge at Wings seem like a pretty good sort?"

"I'd say so," Rette replied. "Wouldn't you, Jeff?"

"Definitely," Jeff agreed.

"What are you flying?" Mr. Wynn asked Rette.

"A Cessna."

"Like it?"

"I've only been up once," Rette said, "but you bet!"

Mr. Wynn glanced toward the stairs, then at his watch, finally at Jeff. "Always late," he grumbled. "Two slowest females in Avondale. Elise!" he bawled in a voice that vibrated against the walls.

"Just a minute!" Elise called back from somewhere up-

117

stairs. "I'll be right there." But it was a good five minutes before Elise and her mother came downstairs together, smiling and serene and unperturbed that they had kept anyone waiting.

Mrs. Wynn wore a black dinner dress, slim and sophisticated, and Elise held up the skirts of a pink-and-white candy-striped taffeta, with a dust ruffle of vivid green. With her fair hair falling to her shoulders and her young shoulders creamy against the silk, Rette thought she looked more like a fashion model than a mere senior in Avondale High.

Elise caught the glance of frank admiration and smiled at Rette. "You like it?" She whirled around, making the skirt flare. Then she laughed at her own conceit and wrinkled her nose at her audience. "It's new," she told them. "I just have to show it off."

Mr. Wynn grunted something intended to be appreciative as he helped his wife into her wrap and shrugged into a gabardine topcoat, but he didn't really see the women's clothes. "Elise," he said as he picked up his hat from the hall table, "know who's teaching your friend here to fly a plane? Patty Creatore."

"Pat?" Elise cried. "She's wonderful! I've met her."

Mr. Wynn tapped his hat thoughtfully against his hand. Then he seemed to make a decision. "How'd you like a course of lessons for a graduation present, Lise?" he asked his daughter.

Elise turned, her eyes widening, quite overcome. "Daddy! Do you mean it?"

"Carter—" Mrs. Wynn started to protest, but her husband waved his hand imperiously.

"Been thinking about this," he said, "for quite a while. If Pat Creatore and Stephen Irish are both out at this new airport, that's a good enough recommendation for me. And here's a girl to talk flying with, besides. The time is

118

ripe. You think it over, Lise, and if you want the lessons more than some folderol like a wrist watch or—or whatever girls get nowadays—you may as well begin next week."

Elise was so astonished that she couldn't find adequate words in which to say thank you, but she crossed the hall with flying steps and flung her arms around her father's short neck. Carter Wynn, pleased but a little embarrassed by such demonstrativeness, grinned at Rette and the boys over Elise's shoulder and carelessly slapped his hat on the back of his head.

"Let me go, Baby!" he told her boyishly. "We're late, and so are you kids." He shook hands hastily with Jeff and Larry. "Have fun," he called back over his shoulder as he followed his wife out of the door, "and get the girls home at a decent hour."

"We will," Jeff told him. "And now let's get going," he suggested to Elise. "You can enthuse as we ride along."

Sitting on the back seat of the car beside Jeff, Elise kept saying: "I just can't believe it. I never dreamed!" For the moment the surprise of her father's offer overshadowed the coming party and everything else.

Jeff was rather quiet, but Larry teased. "I can't see you flying an airplane, Elise. If you want to go in for sports, why don't you do something decorative? You'd be a knockout on an aquaplane."

"See you in the Sunday supplement," Elise retorted, but her mind wasn't really on the repartee. She sat with her hands clasped tightly around her little evening bag, looking like a Meissen figurine but with a light in her eyes that Rette recognized. Temporarily Elise had left them; she was living in a world of dreams.

Her social conscience began to return as they approached the high school, however, and Elise walked up the broad stone steps beside Jeff, talking and laughing

119

with her customary poise. With Rette, she went to the girls' locker room to drop her coat and give her hair a final inspection. Then, just as they were about to turn away from the mirror, she caught Loretta's eye.

"You aren't—mad?"

"Mad?" Rette pretended to be nonplused. "Why should I be?" Yet a nagging imp of jealousy belied her tone. She was ashamed of herself, but she couldn't help feeling a little resentful that Elise should so neatly steal her thunder. It was natural that Rette should consider the flying lessons something special, something apart, something that was hers alone. And now she would have to share the thrill, the interest, the acclaim . . .

"Daddy's so—impulsive," Elise said slowly. "When he wants to give me something he never thinks how it looks."

Rette knew that Elise was concerned because her father's manner of making the gift might have seemed arrogant or self-important. But she didn't try to reassure her. She just stood and waited for her to go on.

Elise's next words came as a surprise. "Jeff ought to try to get a job out at the airport, afternoons and Sundays," she said firmly, her attention no longer directed toward Rette. "Maybe he could save enough money to take some flying lessons himself." She sighed. "Oh, I don't know! I'm all mixed up." Then, noticing Rette's puzzled expression, she added: "It doesn't seem right, somehow, that I should just have things handed to me. In comparison, Jeff has so little." Abruptly, as though she had already said too much, Elise stopped.

But Rette picked up the last word. "Little?" It seemed to her that Jeff Chandler had a great deal—a big position in the class, a way with girls like Elise, brains along with some very attractive brawn.

Elise met Loretta's eyes. "Jeff and his mother have a pretty rough time. You know his dad died years ago, and

Mrs. Chandler does monogramming and fancy sewing for a big store in the city. Haven't you ever met her? She's awfully sweet."

Rette shook her head. She had never met Mrs. Chandler, nor had she realized that Jeff's lot wasn't easy. But Elise had explained a good many things—the reason Jeff had taken the tutoring job, the reason the flying prize would have meant so especially much. Come to think of it, too, Jeff had always worked on a grocery truck, summers. He became, seen in this new light, more real in Rette's eyes, less a superior being. He had problems—different from hers, but still problems. She could understand him better now.

Voices, raised in laughter, drifted through the swinging door. "Come on!" Elise said. "You'd better get out to the ticket table, Rette. People are beginning to come."

To be chained to the ticket table for a full hour and a half was a chore to which Dora Phillips would have submitted only because it gave her prestige as a member of the Senior Ball committee. But it suited Rette right down to the ground. It gave her something to do with her hands, and it used up the awkward part of the evening—the time when girls inevitably congregated in the locker room or in little knots in the gym, waiting for the party to get going without making much effort to start it off.

Of course, now that they were seniors, there wasn't the protracted period of horseplay to live through; the boys were older, more assured. It wasn't necessary for a chaperone to round up the stragglers and blow a whistle for a Paul Jones. Elise and her helpers could be counted upon to see that things ran smoothly enough.

Larry, with customary nonchalance, had disappeared the moment the girls had left their escorts to go into the locker room, and Rette didn't see him all during the time she sat in the hall taking tickets and making change for

121

the stragglers who were paying on the spot. When it became quite obvious that even late-comers had checked in, Rette stacked the tickets neatly in their box and prepared to close up shop, though she felt reluctant to join the noisy crowd in the gym.

Suppose nobody asked her to dance? Oh, Jeff would get around to it, probably, because he had a certain obligation. And Corky Adams would want to hear about the flying lesson. But suppose Larry avoided her all evening, in payment for being practically forced to drag her along? He was capable of such treatment, Rette could believe. She frowned and shivered, feeling suddenly chilly in the empty hall.

The gym doors opened, and Elise swished through, with Dick Sharp at her heels. "Why, Rette! What are you doing out here? I thought you had finished long ago!"

Rette made a feeble excuse, embarrassed because she was afraid Elise suspected the real reason for her delay. "I was just coming," she said. "But first I'll have to drop this stuff in my locker, to be sure it's safe."

In the locker room she dawdled, repowdering her nose, chatting with a couple of girls who wandered in. But eventually she had to go into the gymnasium, alone.

She chose a time when there was a break in the music, and slipped through the swinging doors as inconspicuously as possible, sliding along the wall in search of some friend she could join. Couples were sauntering off the floor, and it was Judy Carter who hailed her, running forward with little bouncing steps.

"Rette, I've got to talk to you! Isn't it too divine about Elise? And she's been telling me you've actually been flying a plane *yourself*. I want to hear all about it, but everything!"

Judy's partner trailed in her wake, interested too. It was a novelty in Avondale for a high-school girl to be learning to fly. And now that Elise Wynn planned to take it up, the interest had doubled. Several other heads turned at Judy's cry, and before she knew it Rette was the center of a group.

"But isn't it hard?"

"How do you feel?"

"Aren't you scared—now tell the truth?"

The girls' questions seemed silly to Rette, but the boys asked sensible things.

"Are you flying a Cub?"

"Who's your instructor?"

"How many hours before you can solo?"

Rette, hesitant for the first few moments, soon found herself talking as spontaneously as though she were at home. The girls were interested in emotion, the boys in action. And until Elise had actually done some flying, it was Rette Larkin who could give them the real low-down on some things they wanted to know.

When the couples began to drift back to the floor Loretta knew a moment of panic. Suppose she were left all alone? But then Chet Currier, a boy with whom she had never exchanged more than half a dozen words, asked her to dance.

Chet wasn't a glamour guy, but he did nicely for a start. He danced rather heavily but with direction, so that Rette's unfortunate tendency to lead was overcome by sheer force. With the next break in the music Chet delivered her back to the side lines, but Corky Adams was there waiting, and then, a little while later, Jeff Chandler came up with Larry in tow.

By now Rette had sufficient self-confidence so that her recalcitrant escort failed to intimidate her. When he muttered the thought that they might as well dance, Loretta assented casually, looking neither pleased nor displeased. She hadn't expected the world on a silver platter. She was getting through the evening without being a wallflower and that was enough.

When he led her to the floor Larry was already looking around for a partner to succeed Rette. He took her in the circle of his long arms with bored condescension and languidly started to follow the music, trying none of the trick steps for which he was famous and which had earned him a reputation as one of the best dancers in Avondale High.

Larry didn't start a conversation, so Rette didn't either. She refused to chatter like a silly magpie to a boy who was being supercilious and practically rude. But she did concentrate on her dancing. To the best of her ability she let herself relax, and, under the guidance of a really adroit partner, she found herself responding to the music as she never had before.

Rette had the natural co-ordination, the ease of the born athlete. She could dance, given the opportunity, as she could do most other things that require balance and physical skill.

"Say, you're not bad," Larry admitted after a few minutes.

It was a backhanded compliment, but better than nothing. "You're not bad yourself—only a little monotonous," Rette dared to return, with a grin to soften the barb.

"Oh! So?" Immediately Larry led her through a series of steps that left her breathless. She laughed up at him without constraint now, her eyes sparkling.

"Do that again," she urged the boy. "That's fun!"

It wasn't every girl who could follow Larry Carpenter when he improvised, and Rette wasn't as smooth a dancer as Elise Wynn or Dora Phillips, but she was adequate.

"Very adequate," Larry told her when he left her. "We'll try it again."

He was as good as his word. After Rette had danced with Jeff, and again with Corky, Larry came back and introduced her to still further variations in his technique. Finally he took her back to join Elise and her escort, and he wasn't supercilious now, only faintly condescending, treating Loretta like a little girl in whom he had discovered an inclination that might be developed into a talent some day.

Rette was actually surprised when it was time to go home. She was flushed and excited and prettier than usual, with her hair curling in damp tendrils on her forehead and neck.

When she was delivered at her door she thanked everyone warmly, directing her glance especially at Jeff.

"I had a lovely time," she said, and was surprised to find that she meant it.

"Really, I did have a lovely time," she told her mother a few minutes later, sitting on the edge of her bed in the darkened bedroom. "Larry Carpenter is a marvelous, dancer, and he showed me a lot of new steps."

Whispering, so that they wouldn't wake Rette's dad, the two discussed the party. Finally Mrs. Larkin reached out and patted her daughter's hand. "You'd better run along now," she said. "It's pretty late." Then, when Rette bent to kiss her, she added, "I'm glad you had fun."

And Loretta, humming softly as she went back to her own room, never remembered that just a week before she had insisted to her mother, "School dances are simply too dumb!"

CHAPTER FOURTEEN

During the next two weeks Rette discovered that there were two entirely different attitudes concerning the art of flying an airplane. Friends of the family met her on the street and questioned her with incredulity.

"Don't tell me you're actually going to learn to fly? But aren't you scared? Well, I don't know—this younger generation—"

Rette smiled and answered them with common courtesy. "It's really lots of fun."

But she found that older people often considered her quite daring and that many of them were ready to insist that she was even foolhardy. More than one friend of her mother's phoned and said: "Nancy, I don't know what you're thinking of. Why, Loretta's just a baby! Of all the ridiculous things—"

Mrs. Larkin and Mrs. Wynn clung together and managed to weather the storm of protest from conservative Avondale, but the censure left scars. Rette's mother began to watch her anxiously, and obviously wasn't sorry when a week of April rain and fog forced both girls to cancel their flying lessons and remain safely on the ground.

Out at the airport, however, the attitude toward flying a plane was completely reversed. It was something that a person did, just as one ate and slept and walked and drove a car. It wasn't considered in the least unusual: it was the norm.

During the week of rain, Rette, unable to stay away from the airport, did her first "hangar flying," as Pat called the endless discussions of air experiences that go on among pilots or students. She picked up a vocabulary that was new and vivid and fascinating, and showed off extravagantly before her parents and Gramp by using expressions like "prop wash" and "fishtail" and "CAVU."

Before Tony, however, Rette subsided, fearing to be corrected or teased. She was secretly disappointed because Tony showed little interest in her flying. He seemed to be walking around with his head in a private set of clouds these days.

Before the rains descended, Elise had gone up on her first dual hop, Rette on her second. Rette still found it hard to believe that Elise could actually be interested in the business of flying. It seemed so out of character. To Loretta, Elise epitomized everything that was feminine. She reminded her of a line of a song that was popular a few years back:

"The girl that I marry will have to be
As soft and as pink as a nursery. . . ." *

Satins and laces and eau de cologne seemed to be Elise's birthright, not the jargon of the airport and the flying of planes.

She didn't even dress the part of the student pilot. She wore a sweater and a tweed suit on the day she took her initial lesson, instead of the slacks or dungarees Rette affected, copying girl flyers in magazine illustrations she had seen.

Not that slacks were in the least necessary. Sitting in the cabin of the little Cessna was as comfortable as sitting

* Copyright, 1946, by Irving Berlin.

behind the wheel of any car. The only difference was that the plane didn't drive like a car. It sounded like one and it smelled like one and it was even interior-decorated to look a little like one, but Pat had been right in saying that the wing and the wheel were contradictory. Rette was already finding it out.

During Rette's second lesson in the air, Pat taught her to do turns to headings, sighting an object at a 45- or 90- or 180-degree angle to the plane and turning until she approached it, then rolling out. She did some climbing turns too, and just when she was settling back in her seat, feeling rather satisfied with herself and calmly looking out to the right and left as the ground fell away beneath the ascending plane, several things happened in quick succession.

"You're banking too steeply," Pat called. "That's all right in a level turn, but not in a climb." Then, soon after Rette had leveled off, Pat snapped, "Bring your left wing up!" A few seconds later, "Your nose is too low."

It seemed to Rette, in the next ten minutes, that she couldn't do anything right. In her next turn she forgot to neutralize and handled the stick as she would have handled the wheel of her bike, keeping on pulling it around after she was in a turn. Then Pat criticized because she failed to co-ordinate her ailerons and rudder. "You're horsing the plane around too much," she said.

By this time Rette was feeling as jittery as a newly saddled colt. She felt confused and incapable of remembering any of Pat's instructions. Her mental picture of how a plane flies wavered and disappeared. She concentrated so hard on the controls that she became jerky and tense, and Pat rapped out one criticism after another as Rette tried to follow instructions.

"Pull your nose down to the horizon. Look before you make a turn. Don't jerk the stick that way!"

Rette's self-confidence evaporated into the blue air. "Relax," Pat said finally. "I'll take the controls for a minute. Look around and tell me where we are."

Rette looked down on a toy village of neat streets and houses. "Why, we're right over Avondale," she said.

"Where do you live?" Pat asked.

"On Cherry Tree Road."

Pat manipulated the plane skillfully into a quarter turn. "Your house ought to be off the right ring, almost directly below."

"It is!"

Rette wished there were someone in the garden, so that she could wave. The row of maples beside the garage was tinted with green, and the forsythia by the back fence was a blaze of yellow, even from this distance.

But Pat didn't give her long to feast her eyes. "All right, now," she said. "Advance your throttle and climb to two thousand feet."

For twenty minutes longer Rette worked with the intense concentration Pat demanded. She climbed out of the plane finally, spent and unsure of herself. Gone was the exhilaration of the first flight, gone the sense of immense capacity. Rette realized for the first time why flying is difficult to learn—because her instincts, her most deeply established habits of mind and body, kept tempting her constantly to do the wrong thing.

Walking back to the airport office, after leaving the Cessna on the line between a Piper trainer and an Ercoupe, Pat said, "Remember when I asked you to climb to two thousand feet back there?"

Rette nodded.

"You climbed so steeply you came within a hairsbreadth of going into a stall. For a minute I didn't think you'd make it."

Rette looked concerned. "What would have happened?"

"Plenty." Pat grinned roguishly. "Next time we go up we'll try some stalls—not accidentally though—on purpose."

Riding home from the airport, Rette did no singing on this day. Her eyes were thoughtful, and for the first time in her life she felt abashed at the prospect of being put to a physical test.

Flying she considered a sport, and at all other sports—hockey, basketball, tennis—she was an acknowledged leader. Incited by competition, she had always learned a new game quickly, and she had early recognized the sense of power that comes from conquering an opponent. The thrill of winning could make her eyes sparkle and her blood run quick.

But in flying Rette missed the stimulation of the fight. Each time she went up she came to a deeper realization that this was something entirely different in her experience. Flying was something one did *alone*. There was no competition to spur her on. She would stand or fall on her individual performance, as would Elise.

Rette wondered about Elise and decided to ask Pat, next time she came out for a lesson, how her classmate was getting along. No matter how clumsily she herself handled the controls, Rette was fairly certain that Elise's performance wouldn't match her own. She didn't realize that she was unconsciously seeking a rival, so that she would feel more at home.

When Rette reached the house on Cherry Tree Road, Gramp was sitting on the back terrace on a straight kitchen chair, hauled out in lieu of the garden furniture, which was still stored in the basement under its winter covering of newspapers. His face was turned to the sun, and he was swathed in such a bulky overcoat that he looked like a wise old turtle, sticking up his scrawny neck to peer around.

Gramp nodded and smiled, sensing his granddaughter's mood before she had said a word. "Flying not going so good?"

Rette sat down on the flagstones and hugged her knees. "It's not the flying: it's me," she admitted. Then she tried to explain her difficulty to Gramp. "I seem to have a blind spot. I can't seem to help thinking of the stick the way I think about a handle bar on a bike or a wheel on a car. And it doesn't work that way at all. It looks like a wheel, but it isn't." Then she laughed at the confusion of her own description. "It's hard to explain what I mean."

But Gramp nevertheless nodded sympathetically. "Don't be impatient, Lark," he told her. "It will come." His blue eyes seemed to look back over the years and he chuckled, half to himself. "I remember when I was learning to drive a car," he said. "It's like it was yesterday."

Rette waited, while Gramp paused and reflected. How anything so long ago could seem like yesterday was hard to understand, but she always humored Gramp when he drifted back over the years and tried to follow him on his wanderings, when older people were apt to be inattentive or brusque.

"I had just got my license," Gramp said after a while, "and you can bet I was proud. I was driving down High Street on the way to your grandmother's—we weren't married yet, but we were engaged—when out of Cuthbert Avenue, like a little black beetle, darts one of those electric runabouts ladies used to drive. I wasn't accustomed yet to meeting another car unexpected, and d'you know what I did?"

Rette shook her head. "What?"

"I pulled on the wheel and hollered, 'Whoa!'" said Gramp, "just like I was driving my father's team."

Rette laughed at the picture. "Did you have a smash-up?"

"Nope," Gramp said, almost sorrowfully. "That little electric scooted around the corner and hugged the curb, though, you can bet."

It was hard for Loretta to imagine a time when there were so few automobiles that each was endowed with a personality, as the cars in Gramp's stories always seemed to be. It seemed odd to think of clutch and brake pedals as strangely behaved, hard to understand, tricky to handle, yet that was just the way she herself had been thinking of the controls of a plane.

Rette rocked back and stared out across the lawn. There had been nothing wrong with Gramp's reactions, she decided, only with his intentions. An image in his head had made him see the automobile he was driving as a sort of mechanized horse. Had he seen clearly in his mind's eye the clutch that can disconnect the motor, the brakes that can clamp down on the wheels, he would then have done the right thing instinctively.

"Yes," Rette said out loud. "That's right."

"What?" Gramp asked.

"I was just thinking out loud," Rette told him. "I'll bet, Gramp, that I'm having the same trouble you had. You didn't really understand a car, and I don't really understand very much about how an airplane flies—not really. Maybe if I could get so that I could *see* in my mind how an airplane works, I'd do the right thing just naturally."

"Maybe you would," Gramp admitted. "It's worth a try."

Rette was still busy with the same line of thought when she walked, in the evening, over to Jeff Chandler's house, her math book tucked reluctantly under her arm.

She was going to Jeff's because he had wrenched his ankle sliding home in a sand-lot baseball game, and the doctor had advised him to keep off it as much as possible for a few days. The number of the house, 128 Potter Street, was firmly fixed in her mind, and Rette scanned the plates above the doors of the row of little houses as she hurried along.

The April dusk was soft, and Rette could see a pink reflection from the sunset in the eastern sky. The trees on Potter Street were few but old, and they bent kindly over the weathered houses, shading the high front porches with their delicate new leaves.

"Rette! Hi, there!" Jeff's whistle stopped her, and Loretta turned up a short cement walk. Using a cane, Jeff hobbled across the narrow porch to meet her. "It was swell of you to come here."

"I don't mind a bit," Rette said honestly. "Except that it's too nice a night to do math."

Jeff grinned. "Are you right!" he agreed. "Let's get it behind us in a hurry." He held open the door.

The living room Rette entered was small and square and lacked the welcome of a fireplace. A bridge lamp turned on beside an overstuffed chair, shone on the bent head of a spare, neat woman who was threading a needle with mercerized cotton. For a second longer she concentrated on what she was doing. Then she looked up quickly and smiled.

"Mother, this is Rette Larkin."

Rette thought she had never seen a kindlier smile on a person's face. Mrs. Chandler's eyes were shaded by glasses, but her mouth was warm and generous and so expressive that Loretta liked her immediately.

"Rette," she said, holding out her hand. "How do you do? Jeff's been telling me about you."

"About what a dummy I am at algebra?"

"About how bright you are at writing! And now I hear you've won the flying prize." She glanced briefly at her

133

son. "I suppose learning to fly is every young person's dream."

"It's wonderful," Rette admitted with an inadvertent catch in her voice. "Now don't get to talking shop," Jeff warned his pupil. "You're here to work." He turned on the light above a round dining-room table and drew up two chairs.

"Talk to me later," Mrs. Chandler urged, settling back in her chair with a square of linen in her hand. "I want to hear all about it, firsthand."

Loretta and Jeff worked for nearly an hour. Then Jeff leaned back in his chair and said: "I'm giving you up—as of tonight. You ought to be able to breeze through any algebra test now, Rette. You've really caught on to what it's all about."

Rette grinned shyly and nodded. "I even feel different about it." She sighed reminiscently. "But it took an awful lot of doing."

Jeff laughed. "I guess anything important usually does."

Rette's mind flashed to her flying lessons, and she nodded. Then she snapped her fingers. "Say, I almost forgot! There's a little lunchroom, for soft drinks and sandwiches, opening in the wing of the farmhouse where the flight office is. I thought you might like to know."

"Me?"

"I was thinking there might be a job—" Suddenly Rette stopped, conscious of what a poor substitute for the real thing she was offering to Jeff—a chance to watch the planes take off and come in when what he wanted to do was to fly. A flush crept up her neck, and she pushed back her chair and started toward the living room. "Skip it. Maybe I've been talking out of turn."

But Mrs. Chandler had also heard. "A job for Jeff?" She looked at her tall son. "That might be interesting—

or at least more fun than driving a truck for the Avon-dale Market. Mightn't it?"

"It might," Jeff agreed, and Rette knew that he was thinking that to be close to his heart's desire would be something—even if the nearness was purely physical—a spot on the other side of a lunch counter that catered to the flyers and students at Wings. At least he could hear the jargon of the air; at least he would get a chance to meet the pilots and plane owners. And—who could tell? —perhaps he might even get an occasional chance to go up.

With the realization that Jeff wasn't offended, Rette's discomfiture evaporated. "If the man needs a helper, it would probably be for afternoons and week ends," she said. "They're the busy times."

Jeff raised a finger. "I'll mush along out there and investigate, Rette. Thanks for the tip." Then he asked, "How are your lessons going by now?"

"I've only had two," Rette said modestly, but the Chandlers began to ask questions, and within five minutes Rette found herself talking unrestrainedly to Jeff and his mother. In the eyes of both there was a light of interest so utterly genuine that she couldn't fail to respond.

"I don't want to make the same mistake I did in math," Rette confessed. "I want to get my fundamentals straight at the start. And I feel there's a lot more I ought to know about how a plane flies—and why. I wish there were a book—"

"But there is!" Jeff cut in. "Haven't you ever heard of *Stick and Rudder?* I understand it's practically the bible of beginning flyers. Ask Tony about it. He may even have a copy, Rette."

So when she went home Rette did ask Tony. He was lying full length on the sofa, listening to the radio, and he shouted above the music, "Sure. Look in my bookcase upstairs."

Rette found a well-thumbed brown book, scrambled into her pajamas, and lay across her bed flipping through the pages. When Tony came upstairs, he poked his head into her door.

"Make anything out of it, Small Fry?"

"Not much," Rette admitted. "It looks more complicated than college chemistry."

Knowing his young sister's aversion for math and all allied subjects, Tony tried to be consoling. "Start at the beginning. Read a paragraph at a time. Take it slowly. You're always in such a rush."

Then, as though it had suddenly occurred to him, he came in and sat on Rette's window seat and started to quiz her about flying, much as Jeff had. But instead of talking about herself, Rette found that she wanted to talk about Jeff. She told her brother about his enormous desire to learn to fly, about the feeling that was almost like a sense of guilt which attacked her at intervals because she had won the prize, and not he.

Tony looked at Rette, sitting cross-legged on the bed and leaning forward, her elbows on her knees, intense and earnest. He smiled gently. "I think you kind of like the guy."

Rette's flush was hot and immediate. "Don't be silly," she shot back. "Jeff goes around with Elise Wynn."

"Variety is the spice of life," Tony quoted, his eyes twinkling.

"You don't seem to think so."

But Tony only winked. "Tell you what I'll do for your boy friend," he said. "I'll take him up with me a couple times—I'm qualified to instruct—and if he's got any natural ability, it'll show up fast. Then we can go on from there." He unwrapped his long legs and stood up, grinning at Rette's look of astonishment as he sauntered out of the room.

Rette jumped off the bed and ran to the door the instant she recovered. "He's not my boy friend," she insisted, "but, golly, thanks, Tony. Jeff will be thrilled to death."

It was only after she had gone into the bathroom and started to brush her teeth that she suddenly stopped and stared into the mirror. "Well, I'll be darned!" she muttered. "The way men hang together! My own brother, and he wouldn't do as much for me!"

CHAPTER FIFTEEN

Rette sat on the grass in front of the office at Wings Airport and watched Elise Wynn walk across the field with Pat Creatore toward the same Cessna trainer in which she was scheduled to go up an hour from now.

It was such a beautiful May morning, sunny and unseasonably warm, that she had come out early to the airport just to *be* here, just to sit in the sun and soak up the color of the scene—the line of varicolored planes, the busy mechanics in their white coveralls fussing over a ship under repair outside the hangar, the occasional arrival or departure of a trainer like the one Elise would fly.

There was also the chance—Rette refused to admit it as a hope—that Jeff Chandler might steal a few minutes away from his new job and stroll over for a chat. Rette glanced back toward the converted farmhouse, then looked away again quickly, shading her eyes with one hand as she followed Elise to the door of the Cessna's cockpit. She heard the click of the door as it shut on Elise's side, then knew, from the pause in operations, that Elise was doing her ground check. The boy was waiting near the tip of the propeller until he got her signal to swing it through.

"Contact," came Elise's voice faintly.

"Contact!" the boy called back, grabbing the tip of the propeller.

The engine caught instantly, the boy kicked away the chocks under the wheels, then jumped back, and then the sound of his "All clear!" rang above the roar of the motor.

Elise taxied to the runway in the shallow S-turns both girls had learned before their first orientation hop, and Rette still kept her eyes shadowed by her hand as she watched the take-off. It was smooth; there was no doubt about it. Rette wondered how much the instructor had to do with its ease, how much correction Elise needed in her manipulation of the controls.

This was Elise's third lesson, Rette's fourth. On her third trip upstairs Rette had practiced climbing turns, S-turns, and rectangles. She watched Pat and Elise fly the traffic pattern and start for the practice area, visualizing what they would do next.

When the plane was only a spot in the distance, she jumped up, dusted off the rear of her knee-length shorts, and strolled back toward the porch of the farmhouse, pretending that the grass was too damp to be comfortable, but knowing secretly that she was hoping for a glimpse of Jeff.

She even had a reason why she might logically want to see him. Tony had mentioned at the breakfast table that he had run into Jeff at the drugstore last night. Rette hadn't wanted to prod her brother's generosity by asking whether they'd discussed flying, but she was nevertheless curious to know.

Two young men, obviously student pilots, were sitting on the porch steps comparing open logbooks. Stephen Irish came to the door briefly, squinted at the sky, and waved to Rette, but Jeff Chandler did not appear.

Loretta considered going to the lunch bar for a coke, decided it would be too obvious, and wandered back to her original position on the grass after she had gone to the bubbler for a drink of water. She looked at her wrist watch. Forty-five minutes to wait.

She didn't really mind. There was a lot to think about these days. Seniors were being measured for caps and gowns, and preparations for Commencement were well under way. Exams would be early for the graduating class, and almost every week now some special assignment was handed to the seniors, tagged with the promise of a Commencement prize.

Spurred by her recent success, Rette had written several essays, on widely diversified subjects. There was one on Martin Luther—a lengthy and, she thought, very erudite job. There was another brief classroom assignment on homemaking, a dull subject if Rette had ever encountered one. Yet she did her best with the writing, because the winner would receive five dollars from the Avondale Women's Club, and five dollars would pay for another half hour in the air. The Historical Society had offered a money prize also, for a composition of one thousand words on "Our Town." Rette thought she'd try for that too, if she could find time—not that she really hoped to win, but just to get experience, because the more she thought about it the more she felt she might want to major in journalism in college. She hugged her knees and began to dream about a thrilling newspaper career, in which she might conceivably fly her own plane.

"Watching the birds?"

Jeff's voice came from directly over her head, and Rette looked up with a start.

"The big ones," she told him. "Hello."

"Hello," Jeff sat down beside her on a case of coke he had apparently been hauling when he spied Rette. "You flying today?"

"As soon as Elise comes down," Rette told him. Now that Jeff was beside her she couldn't find a way to ask about his meeting with Tony. She sat in self-conscious silence, staring at the sky.

A small plane was crabbing along the down-wind leg of the course around the airport, and both Rette and Jeff watched it approach the runway in a power-off glide.

"That Elise now?" Jeff asked, squinting against the sun.

Rette glanced at her watch again. "I don't think so. She's got half an hour to go."

"It's a Cessna," Jeff said as the plane came closer, landed, then took off again at once. "It looks like Elise."

Rette felt vaguely irritated by Jeff's apparent absorption in another girl. "It can't be Elise," she told him sharply. "She's taking only her third lesson. I'm going up for my fourth, and *I* haven't practiced take-offs and landings yet."

"That would be pretty early in the game," Jeff admitted, but his eyes still followed the silver airplane as it flew the traffic pattern and came down rather bumpily on the runway again.

"By cracky, I think that *is* Elise!" he said.

"It can't be!" Rette sounded really annoyed now, and Jeff turned and looked at her curiously.

"There's a chance," he said quietly, "that Elise may be the kind of natural pilot who learns extra quickly. She *could* be doing landings and take-offs this early. People *have*."

Rette's laugh was thin, and her voice, usually so husky, sounded almost high-pitched. "Not Elise."

Jeff's straight, dark eyebrows almost met over his deep-set gray eyes. "What have you got against Elise, Rette?" he asked. "She's always been decent enough to you."

Rette couldn't meet Jeff's level gaze. She picked at a blade of grass, feeling frustrated and misunderstood. All the beauty of the morning faded, and the sun felt hot

and stinging as it beat down on her head. All right. She
had been petty and jealous; she had been catty and mean.
But she didn't intend to admit it, not to Jeff Chandler.
Just when she'd got the one big thing that had ever come
her way, the flying prize, Elise had to come along and
share the glamour. It wasn't fair.

Rette fought for composure. "I haven't got anything
against Elise," she said with lifted eyebrows. "It's just
that it's perfectly silly—" She bit her lip and stopped.

"It's just that it's perfectly silly to imagine that she
could be a better student pilot than you?" Jeff asked.
"Rette, grow up! You can't always be best!"

Rette jumped to her feet, astonished that Jeff should
dare to scold her as though she were a naughty child.
"I'm not going to sit here and have you insult me," she
said.

Jeff's expression was puzzled. "I'm not insulting you,
Rette." He added gently, "I'm just telling you the truth."

To be chided by her mother was one thing, but to be
taken to task by a member of her own generation, and a
boy at that, was both mortifying and infuriating. Rette
stamped her foot from the sheer necessity for physical
release.

"You wait," she said angrily. "You'll see!" Then, leaving
Jeff without a backward glance, she stalked off, head
high, toward the office.

Jeff hoisted the case of coke to his shoulder and followed her, pausing now and then to watch the Cessna,
which was again coming in over the runway for a practice landing. This time, however, the trainer didn't take
off again, but taxied back to position on the line. Just as
Rette reached the farmhouse porch the doors in the cockpit opened. Jeff, who had overtaken her with his longer
stride, tapped her lightly on the shoulder.

"Look at that," he said.

Rette looked back, scarcely believing her own eyes. It was Elise and Pat Creatore who jumped down from the airplane's metal steps and came toward her across the grass.

CHAPTER SIXTEEN

The fact that Elise Wynn was beating her at what she privately considered her own game was one of the bitterest pills Rette had ever been forced to swallow.

All her life she had secretly admitted Elise's superiority in many things—in popularity, in poise, in appearance, even in brains—but in winning the flying prize Rette felt for once that she had achieved something so special and individual that its fruits would be hers alone.

And without apparent effort Elise was sharing the glory. In fact she seemed to be taking the lion's share.

Not that she reached out for it and grabbed, as Rette in her shoes undoubtedly would have done. Elise seemed unaware that Rette considered her a rival in a sport in which there could be no real rivalry. Indeed, she was friendlier than ever before, as though their mutual interest in the air had given Rette and herself a basis for intimacy.

Rette dissembled, smothering an inclination to be sullen and taciturn. When she met her in the school corridors or out at the airport, she greeted Elise with a smile and never for one moment indicated that she was jealous of her superior skill.

But Jeff knew, and Rette therefore avoided him. He came to the house one night to see Tony, and Loretta

dodged upstairs, feigning an appointment to play pinochle with Gramp. Actually she hung around the upstairs hall, trying to hear snatches of their conversation
as it drifted up the stair well. She hoped they would
make an appointment to fly, and was delighted when she
heard Tony tell Jeff he knew of a Cub trainer he could
borrow. Yet a sense of shame kept her from joining them.
She felt she had lost the right to any regard Jeff had
ever held for her. She felt that she didn't even merit
Tony's brotherly interest any more.

Jealousy, most futile of emotions, bred in Loretta a new
sense of inferiority, just when she was beginning to feel
quite a person; just when she was beginning, also, to
acquire a certain social place in the school scheme of
things. She retreated into her shell, hard as a diamond-
back terrapin's, and spent most of her spare time brood-
ing over *Stick and Rudder*, trying to get from the pages
of the book the key to Elise's success.

"You're not doing badly," Pat told her, when Rette complained to her instructor that she felt inadept and clumsy.
"Your reactions to the airplane are perfectly normal.
You're just a little rough with the controls, that's all. Take
it easy. Don't be too impetuous. You're not running a
race."

Rette was practicing stalls, climbing and gliding turns,
and landings now. She liked to land the plane, enjoyed
calculating to a nicety the glide with which they approached the runway, and was proud that after a couple
of trials she rarely bumped off the ground after settling.
Pat's "Good landing!" was frequent enough to be music
in her ears.

Daffodils were fading in the gardens of Avondale, and
the dogwood was in full bloom by the time Rette went
up to three thousand feet to do her spins.

"Tell me if you begin to feel a little green," Pat warned. "Getting airsick is no fun."

"I think I'll be all right," Rette told her, but she didn't feel as confident as she sounded.

There were two parachute packs in the plane in place of the usual back cushions. "Slip your arms into this harness," Pat said to Loretta. "It's just a formality, really. A spin is rather a simple maneuver."

"Oh, yeh?" Rette said inelegantly to herself. Aloud she asked, "Has Elise done her spins yet?"

"Just yesterday."

"Funny. I saw her at school today and she never mentioned it." Rette looked inquiringly at Pat, but the instructor, busy with the clips on her own harness, didn't seem to hear.

Two small boys in corduroy pants, who had obviously come out to the airport to see the sights, drifted over and watched Rette struggling with her own parachute straps.

"Gee, girls!" one of them said. "D'you spose they're stunt flyers?"

"Betcha," his friend replied.

Their admiring glances made Rette feel like a veteran pilot as she climbed into the plane beside Pat. But a second later the boy who was standing by to prop took the wind out of her sails.

"Naw," he told the kid over his shoulder. "Pat Creatore's just taking up a student for her spins."

"We'll climb a little above three thousand," Pat told Rette as they taxied over to the runway. "You need plenty of altitude, because even in doing a two-turn spin you'll lose five hundred feet—maybe more."

Rette's stomach felt tight as the instructor explained the maneuver. "It's hard to put these planes into a spin, and they recover by themselves after two turns. They're made that way, for safety's sake. But you've got to know how to recover in case you go into a spin accidentally, through misuse of your controls."

"I see," Rette said, trying to sound calm.

As they flew at cruising speed toward the practice area, Pat explained that a spin is always preceded by a stall. "The instant you feel the stall, press your right rudder sharply forward, pull the stick back all the way, and hold it there. The plane will fall off toward the right wing and, with the nose pointing straight down toward the earth, we'll start to rotate to the right."

Rotate seemed a mild word for what Rette knew would happen. She gulped and nodded, trying to listen carefully as Pat explained the method of recovery. "This is one time you should move the controls sharply. You ought to be good at this."

Rette grinned rather ruefully, knowing that a tendency to slap the plane around was her chief weakness. "I'll bet," she said.

Under Pat's direction she climbed to the required altitude. Elise got through it, Rette was thinking, so I can. She tried not to seem nervous but the palms of her hands were wet and so were her armpits. She kept watching the altimeter anxiously: 2800, 3000, 3100.

"All right," Pat said as casually as though she were discussing winding a ball from a hank of knitting yarn. "Let me have the controls now. You follow me through."

She chose a fix point, made sure there were no other airplanes below, then began to climb into a stall.

Rette watched the stick coming back toward her under Pat's practiced hand. Back, back, back—

"Here's the stall!" Pat called.

Down went the nose of the plane. Pat kicked the right rudder sharply. Around went the plane, falling through space, nose down, like a conical top!

Rette conquered a tendency to clutch at the wheel

before her. Wind roared past the struts, and the earth below whirled like a motion picture gone wild. Upside down. Right side up. Sideways! Rette felt her neck jerked around like a flower in a storm.

Suddenly the left rudder moved under Rette's foot, and she could see the stick follow it forward. Pat neutralized the controls after the spin broke, and the airplane went into its recovery dive.

Back on the stick. Easy. "There!" The plane leveled off and Pat glanced at her pupil.

"See?"

"Whee!" as Rette's head cleared, she glanced at the altimeter. They were flying at a little over two thousand feet. She heaved a sigh of relief and relaxed. "See what?"

"See how simple it is to bring a plane out of a spin?"

"Simple!" Rette snorted.

Pat grinned at her. "Feel all right?"

"I'll live," Rette said without much conviction, then added prayerfully, "I-hope-I-hope." Then she grinned back at Pat. "What I'm wondering is how I'll ever have enough presence of mind to pull out of a spin by myself."

"You'll be all right," Pat assured her. "Your reactions are plenty fast." She checked the sky below, then started to climb again. "I'll tell you a modern nursery rhyme:

'In a spin
   If you're in doubt
   Just nose her down
And she'll come out.' "

Rette laughed. "Where did you learn that?"

Pat shrugged. "Haven't the foggiest notion." She glanced at the altimeter needle. "I'll do one more. Then you can try a couple. O.K.?"

"O.K.," Rette agreed. During the next spin she made a

determined effort to follow through on the controls during recovery. If she had to do this trick herself, she decided, she'd better get wise.

Again she was dizzy, again her stomach seemed to be wrapping itself around her backbone, but on the next climb upward she realized with some astonishment that she hadn't been frightened, exactly. The merry-go-round feeling in her middle disturbed her, but that was simply a physical reaction to the crazy tilting of the earth. Actually she had complete confidence in Pat and in the plane.

"Ready to try a right spin yourself?" Pat asked after a minute or two of level flight.

Rette nodded. She was reviewing in her mind each step of the maneuver, trying to make sure that when the time came she would be ready with the proper moves.

"All right. Check for traffic below. Then line up with that railroad track."

Rette felt as though she were about to go off a high diving board for the first time, but she did as she was bidden, then nudged the plane up into a stall and kicked the rudder. Fortunately now that she was operating the controls herself, her body was not tense. She possessed the fine quality of relaxation when in action, that quality which makes great athletes. As the plane went into its spin she counted out loud.

"One! Two!" Her recovery dive was steep, her pull-up a little too sharp, but there was no indecision in her reactions. Her parted lips and shining eyes told Pat how much she was enjoying the excitement of it.

"Good girl!" the instructor called.

"I ought to try it once more," Rette said of her own accord, ignoring her still rebellious stomach.

Pat nodded. "Try a left one this time," she said, "and watch your stick pressure more carefully."

Rette nodded, and as the plane again winged over into

its spin she noticed that her head was clearer than before, that the feeling of dizziness was gradually vanishing. She executed the maneuver with more precision, and Pat seemed very pleased.

"Feeling a little less whirly?" she asked.

"Much less."

"Fine." Pat wanted to show Rette some accidental spins, so that she would know what can happen when a plane is flown carelessly or pushed beyond its capacity. They climbed back to three thousand feet and worked for fifteen minutes more before it was time to call it a day.

Back on the ground again, Rette felt proud of herself. She knew that she had come through with a good show, and she felt as she did after helping to win a particularly tough basketball game for Avondale—except that in the air she was the whole team.

If her knees were a little wobbly as she walked away from the plane, she concealed it well. Her head was high and her eyes were still bright with excitement as she handed Pat her logbook and watched her write in it.

"Stalls and spins . . . total time: 8.15." Pat slapped the book shut, gave it back to Rette and said: "I'm thirsty. Come on over to the lunchroom and I'll buy you a milk shake or a coke."

It was the first time Rette had ventured into that part of the building since the day Jeff had scolded her so roundly because of her attitude concerning Elise. She followed Pat reluctantly, more because she couldn't think of a convincing excuse than for any other reason, and wasn't particularly surprised to see Elise herself sitting at one end of the counter, chatting with Jeff and a young instructor whom Rette knew solely by his first name, Eric. Both Eric and Elise were eating hamburgers and drinking big glasses of milk.

"Hi!" Eric called, turning as he saw Pat come through

the door. "I'm stealing one of your pupils. Going to give her a ride in that new Bonanza. O.K. with you?"

Pat looked at Elise, and her eyes began to twinkle. "Don't trust him," she warned, then dodged as Eric threw a wadded paper napkin at her head.

Jeff came over as Rette and Pat climbed up on two stools, and put both palms professionally on the counter. "What can I do for you?"

"I want a coke," Pat said promptly. "How about you, Rette?"

"I don't want to be a pig, but I'd love to have a milk shake."

Pat nodded to Jeff. "Strong stomach. Rette's just been doing her spins."

Overhearing, Elise looked interested and leaned forward. "Have you, Rette? How did you make out?"

"Ask Pat," Rette advised.

"She did swell," Pat said ungrammatically. Then her tone became bantering, "And I must say it was a pleasure, Elise, after you."

Elise waved at Pat like a kitten batting at an adversary, but didn't say a word.

"Why, what happened?" Rette's question was spontaneous. She felt completely in the dark.

Elise bowed her head sheepishly. "I just lost my lunch, that's all."

"That's all," Pat agreed. "And at least she had the good grace to wait until she got back on the ground. I've had students who've been less courteous."

"Well, that's something!" said Elise in a teasing voice. She looked toward Rette and gestured. "Her first kind word."

Jeff put the milk shake in front of Loretta and served Pat her coke. Eric paid for the hamburgers, and he and Elise went out together. After they had left, Pat nodded her head toward the door.

"I think our Eric has a slight crush on your young friend," she said.

Rette glanced quickly at Jeff, but he was busy running water into the milk-shake mixer. He finished washing up, then strolled over and talked to the girls for a few minutes. "That's some kite, that new Bonanza," he said, using the jargon of the airport.

Pat nodded in agreement. "Quiet too." She glanced at her watch and slid down from the stool. "Don't hurry," she said to Rette, who was still sipping her milk shake, "but I've got to go."

Rette was left alone in the lunchroom with Jeff, and as the door banged behind the instructor she felt a little lost. She clung to the subject of the Bonanza for the longest time possible, then said abruptly, "Where's your boss?"

"Gone to town for some supplies," Jeff returned. "Business is picking up. For summer this may develop into a full-time job."

"Would you like that?"

"Sure," Jeff said. "Anything to be near airplanes, you know." He grinned, then as quickly turned serious. "Say, Rette, I want to tell you I think your brother is one great guy."

"He says a good word for you too," Rette smiled back.

Jeff leaned on the counter on both elbows. "Seriously, I think it's pretty swell of him to offer to give me some flying lessons. I mean, I haven't got any way of paying him."

"I don't think he'd do it for pay," Rette said thoughtfully. Somehow, though she had never considered it before, she felt sure this was the truth. "I think you remind Tony of the way he felt when he was in high school. You know he was always crazy about the air."

"I know," said Jeff, "from your flying essay. I read final proof on the graduation issue of the *Arrow* last night. You know I shifted it over to a lead position."

Rette hadn't known, and her emotions concerning the

news were mixed. On the one hand she was flattered, and on the other she felt that the essay was almost uncomfortably intimate, that perhaps it would look a little foolish in print.

"Does it—look all right?"

"Sure, it looks swell. It was a natural for the prize," Jeff said.

But Rette wriggled her shoulder under her checked sport shirt. The fate of the essay, and its eventual publicity, alarmed her vaguely. The fact that nothing is all black or all white, all good or all bad, was something she was coming to recognize, yet it still irritated her. Growing up, she decided as she left the lunchroom and walked around the building toward the parking area, wasn't as much fun as it was cracked up to be.

CHAPTER SEVENTEEN

After dinner that evening Rette walked down to the drug-store to get a prescription filled for Gramp.

Elise was sitting in a booth, idly turning the pages of a new magazine, and she looked up when Rette came through the door as though she were waiting for someone.

"Hello," she said cordially.

"Hi!" Rette replied. She went to the counter at the back of the store, where the druggist peered at the prescription and said, "It will take about twenty minutes," then she wandered back and stood looking down at Elise.

"Do any more spins?" she asked.

"A couple," Elise said ruefully. "I can't say I take to them like a duck to water."

Rette's curiosity got the better of her. "When we were talking in school today, why didn't you tell me you'd been doing spins?" she asked abruptly.

Elise's eyes widened. "I didn't want to scare you," she said as though this should have been obvious to Loretta. "Pat says the worst thing about spins is the anticipation, and I thought if you found out I got airsick—" She stopped and shrugged with a delicate gesture that reminded Rette of Mrs. Wynn.

"Well, that was awfully decent—" Rette said and also paused.

Elise sat back, her fair head against the booth, her arms straight at her sides, palm down on the seat. "I was terrified," she admitted suddenly. "I think maybe that's why I got sick, because today I was all right. The worst was over."

Rette nodded, thinking back on her own experience. She had been nervous, and even scared, but she hadn't felt overwhelming fear. She had conquered no real terror, as Elise apparently had. With sudden perception she realized that the fragile blonde girl before her had been actually brave.

She found unexpectedly that she wanted to reassure Elise, and she sat down on the corner of the opposite booth and said, "Pat thinks you're a better student than I am. I know she does. She says you're smoother and calmer and—and everything."

Elise smiled. "Thank you, Rette," she said. "But I haven't got your drive."

"Pooh," said Rette. "What does drive matter?" She made a major admission. "You'll solo before I do. You wait and see!"

Elise shrugged again. "Maybe. That isn't important, is it?"

Rette, who had been considering it very important, asked in astonishment, "Why not?"

Elise laughed out loud. She leaned forward, her slender hands clasping her elbows, and said: "We're not trying to beat each other at some game. We're trying to learn to fly an airplane safely and—alone."

Elise was right. Reluctant as Rette was to admit it, she recognized that Elise was looking at flying through more mature eyes than she was. Rette had to accord her a certain admiration. Elise was learning to handle a plane as smoothly as she handled boys, and without undue fuss.

Elise probably deserved her spot in the limelight at school. She was actually quite a girl.

For the first time in her life, Rette found herself wanting to be worthy of another girl's friendship. As she sat on with Elise, discussing flying, she became aware of a sense of values more firmly rooted than her own.

"I like to fly," Elise said after a while. "And I like having Daddy so interested. But I doubt if I'll ever go on and learn to navigate or solo cross-country. And somehow I think you will."

"Me?" Rette touched the pearls at the throat of her sweater in astonishment.

"You." Elise said it firmly. "You'll find a way, somehow. You'll *want* to enough." She hesitated, then added, "That's what I mean by drive. I haven't that—" she spread her hands "that *urgency*. It's a great thing!" There was something that touched on envy in her tone.

Rette was so astonished that Elise could find anything enviable in her that she scarcely heard the druggist when he called, "Your prescription's ready, Miss."

She walked over to the counter absently, paid for the bottle of capsules with money from her wallet, and was about to return to Elise when she saw the young instructor called Eric come through the door and hurry to the booth where Elise was sitting.

"Sorry to be late," she heard him say. "I got tied up at the airport."

They were so immediately absorbed in each other that neither Elise nor Eric saw Rette leave the store. She let the swinging door fall back quietly, and walked home through the quiet suburban streets feeling that the world was full of a number of remarkable and unexpected things.

Street lamps winked through the arching trees, splashing light on the cement pavements, and the stir and excitement of spring was in the air. Seed pods, drifting down from the maples, made dark stains like wiggly worms in light places along the road, and the toes of Rette's shoes scuffed against them as she sauntered along.

In front of the Larkin house a car was parked, and Rette quickened her pace a little until she saw that it was Ellen's. Then she slowed and walked sedately past it to the gate, looking the other way in order not to intrude on the possible occupants.

But a voice from the darkness called, "Rette!" and she stopped and turned. "Come here a minute," Tony said.

Rette walked over to the car as Ellen straightened in the curve of Tony's arm. Tony flicked away a cigarette, which made a bright arc in the darkness, and said: "Sis, we want you to be in on something that's to be a secret to the general public for a while yet. Ellen and I are announcing our engagement the first of June."

Loretta wasn't really surprised, and yet it was a shock. She felt a sharp pang of loss, as though she were being roughly torn from her childhood, of which Tony had been such an all-important part.

She was glad that Ellen couldn't see her face when she said, "That's wonderful! I'm awfully glad, Ellen, that it's you."

She meant every word of it, of course. She liked Ellen better than any girl Tony had ever had. She liked Ellen for herself too, liked her quick mind and her ready humor and her patent adoration of Tony. If she had to give Tony over to anyone, she was glad that it would be Ellen Alden who would take him away from the house on Cherry Tree Road. Yet it was hard to give Tony up.

"I'm glad you're glad," Ellen said in her light, sweet voice. "Because I think it will be lots of fun to have you for a sister, Rette."

"For a sister." With those words Rette could feel resentment dissolve. Her brother couldn't always remain her one and only hero: she had other heroes now—Stephen Irish, and, yes, Jeff Chandler. And there would probably be more to come.

"I'm going to have a party," she heard Ellen saying. "Just a luncheon for some friends. And of course I want you to come, along with your mother. You will, won't you?"

"I'd love it," Rette replied. She felt quite grown-up, being thus included. She had never been to an engagement party. It would come at the end of finals, before graduation. So much was happening in so short a time—exams, her solo flight, and now this.

She felt that she should say something else, but was inadept. Twisting Gramp's prescription in her hands she asked nervously, "You've told Mother, of course?"

"Of course," Tony nodded. "She and Dad couldn't be more pleased. I knew they would be. They're as keen about Ellen as I am—almost."

All three of them laughed, and Rette felt more relaxed. "I suppose I should say, 'Congratulations,' or wish you happiness or something. But you know I do." She rested one hand on the door of the car.

Ellen reached out and covered Rette's hand with her own, briefly. "I know you do," she said with warmth. "But don't be surprised, Rette, if it takes awhile to get used to the idea. I'm not completely used to it myself."

Rette found that this was good advice. It was several days before she became really acclimated to the actuality of Tony's engagement, in spite of her parents' enthusiasm and Gramp's repeated assurances that Ellen was "a fine girl." The more she thought about it, however, the more she liked the idea of having Ellen in the family. And Ellen, on her part, treated Rette with such genuine affection that any lingering reservations melted away.

Ellen even consulted Rette and her mother about plans for her engagement party, and the three of them discussed possible ways of announcing the great news and giggled together like three girls. Never in her life had Loretta felt so much a part of things. In fact she felt a little breathless about all that was going on.

Pat Creatore had been out of town, attending the funeral of an uncle in another state, and to Rette it was something of a relief that she wasn't called upon to make her solo flight in the midst of all the rest of the excitement.

But the day came, of course, when Pat returned and phoned from the airport, hearty and full of inducement. "Want to schedule the rest of your lessons, now that I'm back? I've got a couple of hours free Friday afternoon."

Rette thought fast. Ellen's party was Saturday, but Friday was a day completely free, even of exams. "All right," she said hesitantly. "Yes, I think I can make it then."

"I'll call Elise Wynn too," said the voice at the other end of the wire. "Which time do you want—two thirty or three thirty?"

"Three thirty," Rette said.

After Pat had hung up, Rette was a little disappointed that nothing had been said about soloing. Of course there was the chance that she wasn't ready, but Rette had heard enough airport gossip to know that a student pilot's solo flight usually came very quickly on the heels of doing his spins.

Mrs. Larkin, walking through the house with an armful of clean laundry, asked, "Who was that, dear?" as she passed. She was very busy these days, and very intense. She too felt surrounded by activity, with Tony getting engaged and Rette graduating from high school, and the inevitable change-over from spring to summer clothes and household routine.

"Pat Creatore," Rette said.

Something in her daughter's tone must have made Mrs. Larkin stop and balance the laundry on the back of a chair. "I do wish that you'd give up your flying lessons until after Commencement," she said in a voice that sounded slightly harried. "It will only be a couple of weeks—"

"I can't, Mommy," Rette replied, using the old nickname of her childhood. "It would be too long a time between hops. And besides," she added, thinking of an even more convincing argument, "I'm supposed to get more than one diploma at Commencement, you know."

Mrs. Larkin did know, and she also knew that the second diploma to which Rette referred was the Wings Airport testimonial that would accompany the flight certificates. It would be given only if Rette had successfully completed a solo flight.

Rette grinned up at her mother, but the older woman's brow knit in a little frown of concern. "Why there should be two of you in one family," she said as she picked up her laundry and started toward the stairs, "I simply don't know!"

CHAPTER EIGHTEEN

In the Town and Country Shop, on Friday morning, Loretta stood before a long dressing-room mirror trying to decide between a powder-blue linen and a white waffle piqué.

"I like them both," she wailed. "What will I do?"

Mrs. Larkin, in a scrap of flowered hat that made her look young and, as her husband put it, "definitely frisky," sat on a straight chair with her knees crossed and regarded her daughter critically.

"The blue's a lovely color with your skin, and you are bound to get tan, as the summer goes on."

"But the white is so sort of—sophisticated," Rette said. She cocked her head and smoothed the dress over her firm young stomach. "Though perhaps it's a little early for white." She looked up at the salesclerk. "Do you think it is?"

Carefully amenable, the clerk said: "Oh, no, I don't think so at all! They're both lovely on you. I think it's entirely up to you."

"I'll take the blue," Rette decided finally, because she trusted her mother's judgment, when it came to the question of clothes, more completely than she did her own.

"Shall I send it?" asked the clerk.

"Thank you," said Mrs. Larkin, "but we'll take it with

us." Then when the salesgirl had left and Rette was slipping back into her own clothes, she said: "While we're about it, let's see if we can't find some red sandals. They'd be stunning with that shade of gray-blue."

There was one good shoeshop in Avondale, a branch of a big city store, and there Rette tried on some flat red wedges, size 7½, much like the white ones she had worn last summer. They were nice, but somehow not special enough for Ellen's party. She paraded in front of the foot glass, eying them.

"Do you like these?"

"They'll do," her mother said, "but somehow I think it might be fun for you to have some high heels for a change." She turned to the clerk. "Something less bulky, perhaps."

A few minutes later Rette slipped her toes into the softest kid sandals she had ever seen. They were a lovely red, a muted cherry, and they had slender ankle straps and sling backs.

She walked to the mirror, teetering a little because she was unaccustomed to such high heels; but after a couple of turns she quickly found her balance. "They're beautiful!" she breathed.

"They're also expensive," her mother added, "and completely frivolous and impractical." Then she looked at her daughter and smiled. "As a matter of fact they're probably just what you need. I've never seen you look more incompetent and feminine in my life."

Rette laughed out loud, because her mother spoke as though this might be considered a virtue, and the salesman looked utterly confused.

Are they comfortable?"

"Oh, yes!"

"We'll take them," Mrs. Larkin said, and Rette cried, "O Mother, you're a darling! Thanks ever so much!"

"Thank your father," retorted Loretta's mother with a sly lift to one eyebrow. "He pays the bills."

At home, before lunch, Rette put on a fashion show for Gramp. The old man applauded vigorously. "You look elegant," he told his granddaughter quaintly. "You'll outshine Ellen at her own party, you will!"

"Sh!" Rette covered his lips with a remonstrative finger, though she knew it was only loyalty that made him praise her so extravagantly. "Stop teasing me."

Eating French toast and creamed beef with her mother and Gramp at the little table in the dining-room alcove, Rette felt almost tremulous with anticipation. She couldn't sit still after lunch was finished and the dishes were washed. She couldn't find anything to occupy her mind until the clock rolled around from one thirty to three and it would be time to leave for the airport.

Though she didn't voice the thought, because she knew it would only upset the family, she couldn't help wondering whether today would be the day.

By two o'clock Rette was so restless that she started for the airport, riding her shabby bike over the familiar route. The sun, summer-warm, beat down on the top of her bare head and crept into the open throat of her striped cotton shirt. There was a humidity in the air, a heat haze that smacked more of July than of May. She thought of the February day on which she had first traveled this road, packed into a bus with half a hundred Avondale High students. Andy Keller had taken her group on a tour of the place—homely, dependable Andy, whom she now called casually by his first name, just as he called her "Rette," whenever their paths at the airport crossed.

She remembered Stephen Irish's inspirational speech about flying. "The first time you feel that stick move in your hand will be one of the thrills of your lifetime. And when you come to solo—"

163

Rette's heart gave a leap. Very soon now . . . perhaps to-day?

Elise was sitting on the railing of the farmhouse porch when Rette walked around the corner of the building. She was leaning back to look through the window at the office clock. Pat, Rette decided, must be late.

The girls exchanged greetings, and Loretta climbed up on the railing to sit beside Elise, leaning against a pillar and hugging one slack-clad knee boyishly with her arms. "Think you might solo today?" she wanted to ask, but it was an understood thing that students didn't discuss the big day until it was over. Instead she said, "What did you do your last lesson, besides practicing spins?"

"Slips and forced landings and a few steep turns."

Rette whistled. "I haven't done any slips yet." That meant, probably, that she wouldn't solo today after all. She couldn't decide whether she felt disappointed or relieved.

"How many hours have you had now?" Elise asked.

"Almost nine. How many have you?"

"Just nine," Elise answered. "I thought I must have just about caught up to you."

"Hi!" came Pat Creatore's cheerful voice as the screen door to the office banged behind her. "Sorry to keep you waiting, Elise." She touched Rette's shoulder. "See you later, gal." Then she turned to Elise again. "Have you signed in?"

Everything seemed to be in readiness, and Rette watched instructor and student walk together over the turf to the trainer lined up between two Piper Cubs. Pat climbed into the cockpit on one side, Elise on the other, and Loretta couldn't help being just a little bit glad that Elise wasn't going to solo today either. But she knew it for a mean and silly sort of pleasure, and tried to still it by reminding herself that it didn't matter, really, who soloed first.

Rette watched Elise as she S-taxied neatly to the east-west runway and headed about into the wind. She took off, climbed to five hundred feet, and made her first 90-degree turn in the traffic pattern. Well, Rette thought, that's that.

Climbing down from the railing, she walked across the porch and turned her attention to a Seabee monoplane that was being gassed up close to the hangar. Stephen Irish came out on the porch after a few minutes and looked the Seabee over too.

"That job has a water rudder, you know," he told Loretta. "Ever see one?"

Rette said she hadn't, and Irish went on to explain that it was synchronized with the air rudder and operated by the same controls. "Come on down," he suggested. "I'll show you."

For the next ten minutes Loretta was absorbed in her mentor's explanation of how an amphibian operates. She didn't see Elise's trainer come in for a landing, then turn and taxi back to the head of the strip. Rette was walking back toward the office, deep in conversation with Mr. Irish, when she came face to face with Pat Creatore.

"Where's Elise?"

Pat jerked her head toward the sky. "Up there."

Rette shaded her eyes with her hand and looked upward, squinting against the sun. Sure enough, the little Cessna was just flying the down-wind leg of the airport pattern. It made her stomach do double flips to realize that Elise was up there—alone.

With so little fanfare, without blowing of trumpets or wringing of hands, it had been accomplished. Pat must simply have got out, after Elise finished a landing, and walked away.

Stephen Irish was looking at the sky too. "That Carter Wynn's daughter?"

Pat nodded.

"How many hours has she had?"

"Nine."

"In a Cessna? Not bad," Mr. Irish murmured. "Must take after her old man."

"She's a pretty cool customer," Pat told him. "Mild on the surface but quick to catch on, like her dad, and very smooth in her reactions."

"Smooth is a good word," said a voice behind Rette, and she turned to look into the laughing eyes of the young flying instructor called Eric. He seemed to know what was happening, because he looked over Rette's head and spoke to Pat.

"You think the little gal's safe up there alone?"

There was a general laugh, and Stephen Irish said: "Probably as safe as you were on your first solo, son. Most of us just muddle through it, I guess."

"Elise won't muddle," Pat said confidently. "She's O.K."

Rette had a sudden feeling of obligation to tell Jeff Chandler that Elise was making her solo flight. He'd want to see her come in. She excused herself with a murmured, "I'll be right back," and dogtrotted to the lunchroom door, where she told the news to Jeff.

Fortunately there were no customers at the counter, and he followed Rette out to join the group scanning the sky. The Cessna was quite a distance away now, a mere spot in the blue air above the ridge of trees that outlined the low hills beyond the airfield.

"Isn't she flying sort of low?" Jeff asked.

"It looks low from here," Pat said, as the plane dropped out of sight behind the trees, "but that's because of the ridge. You just wait a sec. You'll see her come out on the other side."

But though Jeff stood with the rest for a full two minutes no silver plane reappeared.

At first everyone was simply stunned. Rette, like the rest, couldn't believe the evidence of her own eyes. Without realizing it, she started to walk forward, as though by getting closer to the ridge beyond which Elise had disappeared she could see better—could see well enough to bring her into view.

"Something's happened!"

Afterward Rette couldn't remember who said it, but the realization seemed to hit everyone at once. Stephen Irish reached in his pocket and threw a set of car keys to Eric.

"Take my car and go by the road with Pat. I'll get the wrecker and call a doc."

For several seconds Rette stood stock-still. She was experienced enough by now to know some of the dangers of the air. Elise had been flying low when last seen. Too low perhaps? Low enough so that when she tried a tight turn she might have stalled and spun in? For an instant Rette closed her eyes, then opened them to see Pat and Eric running around the farmhouse toward the parking area, while Stephen Irish and Jeff had momentarily disappeared.

With automatic desire for action, Rette followed Pat. Uninvited, she climbed into the car after Eric had already shoved it into gear. Pat edged over to make room but she didn't speak. Ignoring the ten-miles-an-hour speed rules posted in the airport area, Eric careened down the rough driveway and into the empty road.

"Moon Creek Road's the shortest," Pat said briefly. "There are fields beyond those trees, you know—part of the Juergens' farms."

Wind whipped Rette's hair straight back as they raced along. Looking toward the airport she could see the wrecking car start out, cutting across an edge of the field, bumping and swaying on the rough terrain. Every minute that passed seemed like an hour. Her chest ached with tension and fear and she kept trying to swallow a rough lump in her throat. Like Pat, she kept sitting forward to scan the sky, hoping against hope for the reappearance of the little plane, but knowing in her heart that the time when Elise should have been gliding in for a landing had long since run out.

"She's so coolheaded," Pat murmured after a while, as though she were talking to herself. "I never sent a student up to solo in whom I've had more confidence."

Neither Eric nor Rette seemed able to find anything comforting to say. Rette was thinking of all the ready-room stories she had heard of light planes spinning in from low altitudes. Height and speed—these were the two safeguards of the flyer. The words "low" and "slow" spelled DANGER in capital letters.

But Elise knew that. Elise must have seen, too, the newspaper story about the Claremont boy, who, in spite of all his training, apparently couldn't resist the almost uncontrollable impulse that sometimes follows a pilot into free air. Like scores of his brothers, he dived at and zoomed above his own home, only to spin in from five hundred feet and end up, nose down, in a mass of twisted metal.

What was it Pat had been saying just the other day? "In nearly 70 per cent of fatal accidents the airplane spins out of a turn and hits the ground with the motor running normally."

Rette shuddered, and clutched the door of the car as Eric took a corner as fast as he dared. The airport was on their left now, and they were traveling at right angles to it, far ahead of the wrecking car and its crew.

"But why would she spin in?" Rette asked out loud.

"She wouldn't," Pat said, frowning. "She's got too much

sense." Pat thumped her knee with her fist as though determined to convince herself. "Elise wouldn't lose her head. She wouldn't! I know."

"Take it easy, Pat." Eric spoke with a calmness the two girls appreciated. It made them both grab hold of their self-control. The car was now approaching the ridge of trees, black against the haze. In a few seconds, Rette thought, we'll see what lies on the other side.

But the ridge was much broader than it looked from the airport. The car raced along the edge of a wood for several hundred yards before the ground dropped off to sloping fields again.

Pat flashed a glance at Rette, her eyes puzzled and stormy, then strained forward to see past Eric and the wheel.

"Look!"

Suddenly Rette felt Eric slap on his brakes, and loose stones from the macadam road ground under the screaming tires. Raising herself up by her hands so that she could see over Pat's head, Rette looked, but all that met her immediate gaze was a cow munching grass behind a post-and-rail fence.

Then she saw Elise!

Elise was climbing the fence a scant fifty yards from the cow, which now and then raised its head and considered the girl soberly. Elise was jerking at her skirt, which had apparently caught on a blackberry bush, but she wasn't looking at the skirt. Not until she recognized the occupants of the car did her eyes leave the cow, and her whole expression was one of apprehension and mistrust.

Eric skidded to a stop and got his long legs from under the wheel with astonishing rapidity, while Rette and Pat tumbled out on the other side of the car.

"Is that thing a bull?" were the first words Elise spoke. They were so anticlimactic that Rette started to laugh hysterically, not really knowing whether she wanted most to laugh or cry. Pat, quite efficiently, was disentangling Elise's skirt, and Eric was pumping the survivor's hand in joyous jerks by the time Rette rounded the hood of the car.

"Where's the plane?"

"Back there." Elise indicated a rise of ground at the extreme edge of the oblong field, in the very shadow of the ridge of trees. The Cessna looked trim and tidy and, as far as Rette could see, completely unhurt.

"But—"

"What happened?"

"My gosh, how'd you ever manage to land her?"

Question piled on question, as Elise jumped down from the fence to the edge of the road and her friends crowded around.

"I was trying to do everything just right," Elise explained, looking at Pat almost apologetically. "It was nearly time to throttle down for my landing glide, and I thought everything was as smooth as could be expected, when all of a sudden the engine just stopped."

"Did you have your carburetor heat on?"

Elise nodded. "I'd just put it on."

Eric looked at her severely. "Are you sure?"

"Positive. It's still on. You can look."

Pat and Eric looked at each other. "Sounds like carburetor ice to me," Eric said.

On the far side of the ridge of trees the wrecking car jounced into sight, spotted the Cessna, and roared toward it. Pat jumped up and down on the road, waving a scarf and calling to attract attention, and the car changed its course and rattled toward them, disturbing the feeding cow, which lumbered hastily out of the way.

Stephen Irish jumped down from beside the driver and picked Elise up in his arms and hugged her. "Boy-oh-boy," he said with youthful gusto, "am I ever glad to see you!"

Jeff, keeping with unexpected shyness to the background, looked glad too. Like Rette, he couldn't seem to tear his eyes away from Elise's heart-shaped face. Perhaps they were both afraid that she was a mirage that would dissolve into thin air.

Again there were exclamations, questions, and Elise's soft voice presenting the same explanation. "I knew I'd never make the airport so I just had to take the chance that my glide would bring me down about here." She looked behind her. "Lucky it was a good big field."

"Lucky too," put in Pat, "that winter-wheat crop had just been harvested."

Elise smiled ruefully. "It was bumpy enough."

Stephen Irish stepped over to the driver of the wrecking car and sent him to check the Cessna. "Bring the report back to the office," he told him. "Jeff and I will ride along with the rest of this crowd if we can all pile in. Both of us have got to get back to our jobs."

CHAPTER NINETEEN

Elise Wynn was the toast of Wings Airport and, Rette felt, properly so. She was as proud of Elise's feat as she would have been of the achievement of a sister. And she felt for her an admiration and affection that was surprising and a little breath-taking. In it not a trace of jealousy remained.

"When a student pilot can make a successful forced landing on a first solo, it's something!"

Pat Creatore had put it succinctly for all to hear. Everybody had to congratulate Elise. Everybody had to pat her on the back or wring her hand, or even hug her, as Stephen Irish had done. Everybody had to repeat the story, confirmed by the wrecking crew, that because the Cessna's heat control was on the fritz, the carburetor had iced up and the engine had simply quit. Everybody had to tell the tale about Elise and the "bull", convulsed with laughter that a girl who had so competently conquered one of the great hazards of the air should immediately afterward become weak-kneed at the approach of a farm animal.

Elise went up again on the same afternoon of her forced landing. "After you fall off a horse, isn't it best to climb right back on?" she asked Pat Creatore. "I'm game if you are."

Rette took her lesson an hour late, and she and Pat reviewed all the maneuvers they had practiced, including slips and forced landings, for thirty-five minutes. Stephen Irish nodded to Loretta when she came through the office to get her logbook. He had been looking at the wall calendar, and he turned from it to ask a question.

"When's your Commencement, Loretta?"

"Two weeks from today."

"You'll be sure to get your solo flight in? This thing hasn't upset you?"

Rette grinned and shook her head. "I wouldn't miss getting that diploma of yours for anything I can think of," she said.

"At-a-girl!" Mr. Irish looked approving. "Wait till you see it!" he teased her. "It's worth working for."

It occurred to Rette, as she stood there, that Elise was qualified to get hers today, along with the verification of her student flight certificate. "Mr. Irish." She took a step forward. "I have an idea." She hesitated, as though she were thinking it out, then continued, "Why, couldn't you give Elise her diploma at Commencement too?"

"I could," said Mr. Irish. "Would you like that?"

Rette nodded, although it would mean giving up her spot in the limelight. Not giving it up—sharing it, she told herself.

"It's sort of an honor," Rette explained to Stephen Irish. "I think Elise would get a kick out of it, and so would her dad."

"O.K. It's as good as done."

"That was darned decent of you," said Jeff Chandler's voice at Rette's elbow as the airport director turned away. He had removed the white apron he usually wore

173

in the lunchroom and was rolling down the sleeves of his shirt.

Praise from a contemporary, and especially from a boy, was so rare that it embarrassed Rette. She shrugged off the compliment and walked to the office with quick steps, mumbling that she had her logbook to bring up to date, and that it was getting awfully late.

Late or not, Jeff was waiting for her in the parking area when Rette came for her bike. Elise had gone long since, driving her father's car, yet of course it was Elise about whom Rette and Jeff thought and talked as they pedaled back toward town. They tried to put themselves in Elise's place, and relived the cutting out of the motor and the forced landing.

"She's got a head on her shoulders, all right," Jeff said.

"You bet she has!" Rette agreed with such vigor that Jeff looked at her quizzically.

"I thought up until today, that you didn't like Elise. Then, when we all thought she'd smashed up, I never saw anybody so scared. You were white as a sheet."

"Up until to-day," Rette said slowly, "I never *let* myself like her. I—I guess I was jealous.

"Why?"

"It would be hard for a boy to understand."

"I'll do my best."

Rette rode in silence for a few seconds, then said: "It's like this. All my life, practically, Elise has been held up to me as an example. 'Elise is pretty. Elise is popular. Elise is a little lady!'" Rette made her voice prissy and precise. "I was—" she hesitated, then forced herself to say it—"I was a tomboy. I was all the wrong things, and Elise was all the right ones. At least that's the way it seemed."

Jeff laughed. "But there's no comparison. You and Elise are as different as day is from night."

Rette's chin shot up. "That's just it!"

Jeff braked, and slowed his bike so that he could row along with his feet on the ground. Rette slowed down too.

"Now don't get jumpy," Jeff cautioned, grinning. "You don't want to be like Elise." He hesitated. "Or do you?"

Rette looked surprised, then probed into her own past. "I guess, really, I always have," she admitted slowly.

"Loretta Larkin, you ought to be spanked." Jeff adopted an affectionate-uncle attitude and stopped dead in the middle of the road, looking at Rette directly, forcing her to meet his eyes.

"I don't see why. *You* like Elise. Everybody does."

"Sure," Jeff admitted. "Sure! But, my gosh, *one* Elise is enough. I like you too. Just be yourself and you'll be all right. You've got a fire and enthusiasm that Elise will never have. You'll go places, Rette, someday."

Rette could feel her heart flutter, for all the world like the wings of a fledgling sparrow she had once returned to its nest. Sitting there in the saddle of her bike, one foot on the macadam road, the other twirling a pedal slowly, she found herself breathing as though she had been running fast. She was full of gratitude to Jeff, although she couldn't express it. In a few words he had given her something she needed badly—something that not even the winning of the flying prize had given her—self-esteem.

"I like you too." The words sang themselves in Rette's head. "You'll go places someday." She felt capable of great things. She was Amelia Earhart, Maureen Daly, Ingrid Bergman. But then she corrected herself. "I am Loretta Larkin," she said aloud.

"What?" Jeff had ridden on, and he looked over his shoulder curiously.

"Nothing." Rette laughed, because she was happy and

at peace and because Jeff looked so completely puzzled. "I was just talking to myself." Then she rode quickly to catch up with him and said, "Don't let's be serious any more. I'll race you to the corner of Cherry Tree Road!"

They arrived breathless, Jeff in the lead. Rette didn't stop to say good-by but kept right on riding, shouting a farewell over her shoulder and adding, "Stop in over the week end if you get a chance."

The minute the words were out of her mouth she was astonished at her own temerity. But Jeff's casual, "I'll do that!" made everything all right.

Rette rode on home and found her mother pressing the dress she was planning to wear to Ellen's party. She came up behind her at the ironing board and gave her a quick, affectionate hug.

"You know, Mommy," she said, "I used to wish I was a boy—but desperately! I don't any more. I think being a girl's kind of fun."

Her mother laughed. "It must be the red slippers."

"Boy!" she said lustily, "I'd forgotten all about those!" Rette opened the cooky tin and helped herself to a handful of sand tarts.

But the next day Rette was very conscious of the high-heeled sandals when she dressed for Ellen's party. They made her ankles look slim and her legs long and shapely. They gave her a sort of sensuous pleasure and made her feel very feminine.

Luncheon was laid for twelve at the oval table in the Aldens' dining room, and the announcement of Ellen's engagement to Tony was made simply with cards attached to the dewy fresh gardenias that lay at each place. Ellen looked appropriately starry-eyed, and she wore a ring of which Rette approved highly—a small, flawless, square-cut diamond set simply in yellow gold.

"It looks just like you!" Rette said sincerely as she admired it. And everyone else agreed.

Ellen's friends were older, but they were charming to Tony's sister, as they were to his mother, and Rette found herself talking and laughing with them as easily as though they were girls of her own age.

Mrs. Alden, a tall, rather queenly woman with upswept gray hair, sought Rette out after luncheon and asked her with interest about her flying lessons. Soon everyone was talking about flying and predicting that, with a husband like Tony Larkin, Ellen would soon be learning to fly. Word had already got around Avondale that Elise Wynn had distinguished herself on her solo flight, and Rette gladly repeated the story, giving Elise her unstinted praise.

When will you solo, Rette?" someone asked.

"I don't know, really. But soon now."

"Soon now" proved to be the following Tuesday. Rette took the last of her exams—in algebra—in the morning and walked out of the mathematics room knowing that she had turned in a good paper. She had recently discovered that it was a satisfaction to be able to *prove* the problems, to be able to know when a solution was right.

Jeff was sitting on the school steps when she came out of the building. He was talking to another boy, but he reached out with one hand and caught Rette's ankle as she was about to pass.

"Not bad, was it?" he asked.

"Not bad at all."

"My star pupil." With his thumb he indicated Rette to the other boy. Then he turned back and looked up at Loretta. "When you take navigation you're going to be able to use that math, young'un!" he said.

"Navigation?"

"Sure. You don't think that when you solo in that kite of yours you're finished, do you? You're just beginning to learn to fly," he teased. Then he asked, quite seriously, "When do you go out to the airport again?"

"Right now. That is, as soon as I grab a sandwich and a glass of milk."

Jeff rose. "Patronize the airport lunchroom!" he said. "I'll escort you there myself."

Daisies were unfolding across the fields as Rette and Jeff rode along the familiar highway. Summer was definitely in the air, and there was no breeze at all. Rette was unusually quiet, because she felt a little sad.

"I won't be coming up here much more," she said after a while. "My ten hours are almost up."

Jeff looked at her out of the corner of his eye. "'Where there's a will there's a way,' unquote."

Rette smiled dreamily. "Maybe you're right," she said.

"Of course I'm right." Jeff was abounding with energy, feeling very sure of himself, very blithe.

"Betcha something!" he burst out.

"What?"

"Betcha by the time we're thirty we both have our own planes."

"Thirty?" Rette was horrified. It seemed impossibly old.

Jeff, understanding, laughed uproariously, slapping the handle bar of his bike. "That's not so ancient," he said. "Gotta have a few years to make some dough."

"I'll tell you something more practical," Rette replied. "We could start a flying club right here in Avondale. Get about a dozen people who like to fly and buy a plane as a group. After we get out of college, I mean."

"You've got something there!" Jeff agreed, and they fell to discussing ways and means, planning ahead with the enthusiastic vigor of youth.

"There's Elise, and you, and me, and maybe Tony and Ellen—"

They still had their heads in the clouds three quarters of an hour later, when Rette had finished her sandwich and the ice cream she had substituted for milk. Pat Creatore stood behind them, listening awhile, then tapped Rette's shoulder.

"Time's awasting," she said. "I thought you came out here to fly, not to dream."

"Can't I do both?" Rette asked her.

"Not at the same time," Pat shot back, "or you'll be a dead duck."

Rette laughed, loving the flip repartee of the airport. She followed Pat out of the lunchroom and over to the plane feeling relaxed and comfortable. As she gave the Cessna the routine preflight inspection she wondered, without urgency, whether Pat would solo her today. It should be today, but there might be some feeling that after Elise's experience Rette might be shy.

"All set?" Pat asked. She glanced down the field toward the wind tee. "What breeze there is seems to be from the south."

Rette took off and landed twice, then started to taxi back to the starting point again. About halfway down the field Pat pressed on the brakes and stopped the plane, then reached down and gave the trim-tab crank a couple of turns to change the flight balance.

"It's all yours," she said quietly, just as she must have said the same words to Elise. "There's one thing to remember. Without my weight the plane will be lighter. It will take off more quickly, and it will hold off the ground longer when you come down." She clicked the door shut, turned her back on Loretta, and walked away.

For a few seconds the "ker*put*" of the idling engine

179

sounded very loud in Rette's ears, and the seat next to her
seemed more utterly empty than anything she could have
imagined. Then, with the airplane feeling very light and
irresponsible, she started to taxi on to the take-off point.

CHAPTER TWENTY

The seniors, capped and gowned, sat in orderly, digni-
fied rows on the big stage of the high-school auditorium,
listening to Corky Adams, their valedictorian, sail through
his carefully memorized speech.

Rette sat with her hands tucked into the wide sleeves
of her gown, comfortably hugging her elbows, and thinking of everything but the future of the socialistic system
in America, in which Corky was apparently intensely interested.

She could see her mother in the fourth row, looking
chic and alert in a new straw hat the color of burnt cork,
with a black rose tucked enticingly under the brim. She
could see her dad, on one side, looking grave but a little
bored, and Gramp, on the other, frankly nodding.

Directly behind them were Tony and Ellen, sitting so
that their shoulders touched and probably, Rette decided,
holding hands. They looked abstracted but very happy,
just as they should.

Ellen wore no hat. A lime-green band the color of her
shantung dress bound her dark, shoulder-length hair, and
her face looked smooth and calm.

She's very pretty, Rette thought. She and Mother are
lovely together—so different, yet both of them so feminine
and smart. Tony and Ellen were talking about an October

wedding, and Ellen had asked Rette to be in her bridal party, but Rette wasn't sure she could manage it, for long ago she had settled on a New England college, and it would be a rather long trip home.

Loretta couldn't imagine, now, that she had ever been even slightly resentful of Ellen. She was just the girl for Tony, the perfect balance wheel, and she fitted into the Larkin family group like a hand into a glove. Gramp was even teaching her to play pinochle, so that he'd have a partner when Rette went off to school.

But then, Rette's feeling about Tony had changed considerably. She still adored him, but she didn't concentrate on him, as she had in the past. To be truthful, she didn't have time to concentrate exclusively on any one thing, not even on her flying. And maybe, she decided as she wriggled in her seat a little, it was just as well, because the flying lessons had, of course, stopped. From now on, she'd have to pay for any future hours in the air out of her own slender allowance.

Loretta saw Ellen lean toward Tony and whisper something. Tony grinned and nodded with a characteristic lift of his eyebrows, and Ellen settled back.

"And I repeat—" Corky Adams was squeaking a phrase that was meant to be thundered, but Rette never found out what he was repeating, for she had drifted off again.

After a few minutes she shifted slightly so that she could see Stephen Irish, who sat with the rest of the speakers and whose name and position were listed on the Commencement program, at once an honor and a stroke of publicity, Rette guessed. Mr. Irish looked very dressed-up, tonight, in a dark-blue pin-striped suit and a white shirt. Rette thought she liked him better in his old Army suntans, which he usually wore around the airport. They suited his bronzed, outdoor look.

She wondered whether Tony would get a kick out of

the fact that she'd get a Wings diploma. He hadn't asked much about her solo flight. It was just as well, perhaps, because even when she had tried to describe her sensations to Gramp, Rette hadn't found much to say. The minute she had got into the air, the worst of her nervousness had disappeared. The plane had semed very light, requiring only the slightest pressure on the stick to make it respond. She had watched her controls especially carefully, and had made sure to keep her nose on the horizon in the turns. Once she had glanced down toward the hangar, where mechanics were moving about their little jobs apparently unaware that a great event was taking place in the sky above their heads. Even Pat, standing in the grass near the landing strip seemed to be looking somewhere else.

Rette remembered most clearly the thump with which the wheels had hit the grass. It wasn't a bad landing. She had made many much more bumpy ones with Pat in the plane to coach her. Apparently her instructor was pleased, because she ran over and called: "Good girl! Now go around and make two more landings, and we'll call it a day."

". . . And meanwhile," Corky was saying, his fist on the lectern, his eye on his notes, "we, the great middle class, are being slowly crushed between the upper and the nether millstones."

Rette shifted slightly so that she could glance down the row on which she sat and see Jeff Chandler's profile. Jeff was looking at Elise Wynn, on the curving front row of seniors, and Elise was apparently searching for someone in the audience. Her big eyes traveled over the auditorium, and her head moved in an inconspicuous quest. The hall was filled, and at the rear of the seats a few late-comers were standing. Rette found Eric before Elise did, standing a little apart from from a sweet-faced elderly couple, looking a bit self-conscious and out of place.

A second later Elise smiled and seemed to relax, settling back in the straight chair. Rette's glance shifted again to Jeff. Did she see his shoulders lift, ever so slightly? She couldn't be sure.

Corky sat down, amid polite applause, and Loretta consulted her program:

VALEDICTORY ADDRESS
PRESENTATION OF AWARDS

She adjusted her collar and tried to look noncommittal, but in her heart she was glad that she would be called to come forward to get her flying diploma. It might be an extracurricular honor, but it could be counted an honor nevertheless. She wished desperately that she could give her family something really big to be proud of—something like the Tate Scholarship—but that was as far beyond her as the nearest star.

Mr. Martin was making one of his usual introductory speeches, clearing his throat and choosing his words with infinite care. Finally, laboriously, he got to the point of saying that it was his very great pleasure to present, in all, twelve awards, including six essay prizes, with which he would proceed first.

"The Dr. J. Will Cheyney prize, for an essay on Martin Luther, goes to Miss Margaret Lewis," intoned the principal impressively, holding out an envelope to Margaret, who looked completely astonished as she stepped forward to take it from his hand.

Rette clapped vigorously. Margaret had worked hard on the essay, she knew. They had met in the reference room of the Avondale Library on several occasions. She was glad to see her come in for a share of Commencement glory, because during all her high-school career Margaret had been such a retiring sort of girl.

". . . On 'Homemaking as a Career'," Mr. Martin was saying, "Miss Loretta Larkin."

Rette started, hearing her own name, and not until she returned to her seat and consulted the envelope did she realize what prize she had received. Then she glanced toward her mother, who was undoubtedly chuckling behind a scrap of linen handkerchief. Rette wasn't surprised. She'd be in for a lot of teasing from the family, who knew only too well that her interests lay elsewhere. Nevertheless the crackle of the five-dollar bill in the envelope was a very pleasing sound.

The D.A.R. medal for a historical essay went to John Hall, which was rather a surprise, as everyone had expected Corky to win it. Then Rette heard her own name again.

"For the essay on 'Our Town,' ten dollars goes to Miss Loretta Larkin, with the compliments of the Avondale Historical Society." Feeling that she had come in for more than her share, Rette again walked to the front of the stage.

Fifteen dollars, in all! Rette couldn't help translating the money into flying time. She was thrilled at getting the two prizes, but she found to her own surprise that it wasn't because of the immediate fame. She was excited by the possibilities that lay ahead.

She let herself dream for a while, as one after another of her classmates followed in her footsteps, then snapped to attention as the really big award, the thousand-dollar Tate Scholarship, was approached.

"This memorial scholarship," Mr. Martin said, "goes each year to the senior whose scholarship, leadership, and athletic ability combine to make a fine all-round student.

This year the choice of the committee of directors was unanimous. It goes to Jeffrey C. Chandler. Jeff—"

Rette's palms stung with the enthusiasm of her clapping. She was so happy for Jeff she could have wept. A thousand dollars! It would be like a fortune! It would smooth the way to a college career, which might otherwise have proved a heavy burden. "O Jeff," she cried silently, "I'm so glad for you, so glad, so glad!"

Rette sat through the rest of the program in a beatific daze. With Elise, she accepted her flying diploma from Stephen Irish, and opened it to find a certificate signed by Pat Creatore and bearing a cartoon illustration, most appropriate, of a frantic fledgling being booted rudely out of the nest. It was just the right touch.

Afterward, at the reception held for the graduating class in the gym, she showed it to her family with amused pride.

"See, it says 'alone and unassisted.' I can hardly believe it myself!"

The flying diploma really meant more to Rette, by far, than either of the essay prizes, and she was surprised by the congratulations these seemed to merit in the eyes of her classmates and her friends.

"So now you have a writer in the family!" Mrs. Wynn came up to say to Mrs. Larkin. Then she turned to Rette. "I read your flying essay in the *Arrow*. No wonder you are walking off with all the prizes, my dear."

"Not *all*," Rette reminded her with a smile.

"Well, it seems to me I heard 'Loretta Larkin' several times."

Tony touched Rette on the shoulder, and Mrs. Wynn turned away to speak to Ellen.

"Hi, Not-so-small Fry," Tony said.

Rette wrinkled her nose at him. "Hi!"

"Got a graduation present for you," said Tony, almost

gruffly. "But it's nothing I can hand to you." He seemed almost embarrassed as he hesitated, then plunged on. "I thought maybe you'd like to have five more hours in the air, with me as your instructor, instead of something like a fountain pen or—"

But Tony never finished the sentence. Right there before a gymnasium full of people Rette flung her arms impulsively around her brother's neck. "O Tony, you know it's the best present of all!" she told him, then stood back a little abashed when he dislodged her arms with a muttered, "Hey!"

Rette glanced around, suddenly self-conscious. Had anyone seen? But all the graduates were busy with their own concerns, and when she met Tony's eyes again he was adjusting his tie and grinning as though he weren't really displeased.

Two flower boxes were thrust into Rette's hands, one long, one short and squat. All over the gym tissue paper was rustling as similar boxes were being opened.

"Eeny, meeny, miney, mo—" Rette counted, and opened the long box first.

There were a dozen roses and a white card reading, "All our love, Mother and Dad." The petals were the color of flame, and the flower stems were very long. Rette drew them out gently, touched and appreciative. "They're beautiful!" she said.

The small box contained a corsage, a modest arrangement of two gardenias, velvet soft, with waxen leaves. On the accompanying card was a teasing message:

"To one of my two best girls—Jeff."

Rette glanced toward Elise, standing with her family not far away. Elise was just pinning a similar corsage to her shoulder, and she caught Rette's eyes and smiled.

"A fine thing!"

187

Rette nodded and grinned back. She was glad Elise didn't seem annoyed.

Jeff himself was unexpectedly at Loretta's elbow, and she thanked him for the corsage but couldn't seem to find any original remark to make concerning the message on the card. Jeff didn't seem to expect her to be witty, luckily, and after a few minutes he said casually, "Take you home after the party, Rette?"

Instinctively, Rette glanced again in Elise's direction. Eric was hovering around her, very solicitous and suave. "I think that would be very nice," Loretta said to Jeff gravely. She didn't mind playing second fiddle. She didn't mind anything any more.

As Jeff turned away, Gramp gave Rette's arm an affectionate squeeze. "Look out, Lark, you'll spill some," he whispered.

Rette turned puzzled eyes toward his. "Spill some? What do you mean?"

"Looks to me as though your 'cup runneth over,'" the old man said.